SHANGHAI EXPRESS

S. Martin Shelton

Inquiries should be addressed to the publisher
Lamplight Press
PO Box 82516
Austin, Texas 78708

ISBN: 978-0-9979774-1-7

Printed in the United States of America
by Lightning Source

Acknowledgements

Danielle Hartman Acee for her text formatting and sage counsel

Michael Cox for his superior China map

Douglas (Doug) Brown for his excellent cover art

Marta Galvan for outstanding copy editing

Bradley Wilson and Mindy Reed for exceptional content and copy editing

Dedication

I dedicate this historical novella to all of the United States Marines and sailors who protected the United States' interests in the Celestial Kingdom during the chaos of the 1920s and 1930s—the period of this story. I especially recognize the ship's company of the gunboat USS Panay (PR5), which Imperial Japanese naval aircraft sunk in the Yangtze on 12 December 1937 in a surprise attack. Four years later, on 7 December 1941, Imperial Japanese naval aircraft, in another unprovoked surprise attack, bombed Peal Harbor sinking five battle-ships, including the USS Arizona (BB39).

Preface

To set the perspective for this tale, let's review briefly the turmoil that riled China at the time of our story: May, 1923. China is in chaos. Since the revolution that overthrew the Manchu Qing Dynasty in 1912, China has had no effective central government. Its leadership of false emperors, military governors, and ineffective republican presidents changes almost yearly due to coups, assassinations, and resignations. Unending internecine warfare rivets the country. Warlords challenge the weak national government: they control entire provinces, key transportation links, and important waterways. Japan and the Soviet Union battle in Manchuria and Inner Mongolia with the goal of annexation.

Bandits roam freely in vast areas of the countryside, terrorizing the rural citizens and raiding Christian missions: theft, rape, pillage, and kidnapping Westerners for ransom is their modus operandi. Pirates raid shipping in the South China Seas. Most national government officials are corrupt. Bribes, threats, and favoritism drive the judicial systems. Students and intellectuals are charged with nationalism, aiming to rid China of Western imperialism and unequal treaties. Mao Tse-tung's Communist party controls Hunan Province and they are forcibly expanding into Nationalist-controlled areas. All manner of corruption rules, and rampant inflation seriously decreases the value of Chinese currency. The Mexican silver peso and the British pound sterling are the currencies of choice.

Whatever law and order there is in China results from the Occidental powers' numerous treaty ports, widespread legations, settlements in major cities, gunboats patrolling the Yangtze and Yellow Rivers, and warships guarding the major ports.

Foreword

I have based *Shanghai Express* on a factual incident. On 6 May 1923, the Blue Express train departed Shanghai at 0900 hours en route to Peiping. At about 0300 hours the next morning, the Chinese bandit Sun Mei-yao and his gang of six hundred brigands raided the Blue Express. The fiction I've incorporated into my manuscript is consistent with the theatre of the times.

In this story, I used the Wade-Giles spelling for all personal and geographical names—as was current at the time.

Cast of Characters

Characters
(in order of first appearance or mention)

Chapter One

    Sun Mei-yao. Leader of the bandit gang (1898 – 1923)

    Fu Kuang-hsǘ. Chinese Mandarin

    Captain Chao Tan-keng. Executive Officer

    Lieutenant Yang Hasi-peng. Engineering officer

    Sergeant Hsu Su-en. Engineer

    Sergeant Tang Tse-che. Squad leader

    Corporal Ts'zo Banh. Machine-gunner

    Colonel Chiang Kai-shek. President of the Wampoa Military Academy (1887 – 1975)

Chapter Two

    Stephan Paskhim. White Russian expatriate

    Mahima Rahman. Senior porter in the first-class coaches

    Margaret Jasperson. Travel agent for American Express in Peiping

    Todd Fleet. Medical doctor and Methodist missionary, with his wife, **Laura**

    Mao Tse-tung. Chinese Communist Party leader and head of the Eighth Route Army (1893 – 1976)

    The *Qizi* (a title). Fu's first wife and head of his household

    Major Quentin Ashley-Cooper. DSO, Royal Marines; British military *attaché*, with his wife, **Karina**

Dino Grandi. Italian Minister of Foreign Affairs (1895 – 1988)

Raymond Poincaré. French Minister of Foreign Affairs and President of the French Counsel (1860 – 1934)

Ramsay MacDonald. Member of the British Labour Party (1866 – 1937)

Lieutenant General Heathcliff Percival-Trengove. GC, DSO. Commandant, British Southeast Asia Command, and Commanding Officer of the Occidental brigade

Captain Sir Mansfield George Smith-Cumming. KCMB, CG. Head of the Secret Intelligence Service (MI6) (1859 – 1923)

Chapter Twelve

Cholmondeley Alastair. Chief of Station, Shanghai, British Secret Intelligence Service

Commander James Stanhope-Owston. DFC, MC. British Military *attaché,* Court of Saint James, Peiping

Mister Carl Crow. Head of the British Red Cross, Shanghai (1884 – 1945)

Major, Sir John Starly. KCB. Secretary of the British Red Cross and negotiator with the Chinese bandits

Chapter Thirteen

Prudence Woodhalm. Cipher clerk in MI6 office in Shanghai

Gwendolyn Llewellyn. Secretary in MI6 office in Shanghai

Edward Stanley. First Secretary of the British War Office (1865 – 1948)

Brigadier General Sir Edward Arthur Fanshaw. KCB. Executive Officer, British Southeast Asia Command (1894 – 1952)

Master Sergeant Shaun McKenna. USMC, Sergeant Major of the Occidental brigade

Chapter Fourteen

Ch'uan Feng. Sun's radio operator

Epilogue

Stanley Wilkerson. Karina Ashley-Cooper's father

Earl of Ancaster Gilbert Heathcote-Drummond-Willoughby. Lord Great Chamberlain (1884 – 1923)

King George V. Regent, British Empire (1865 – 1936)

Major General John A. Lejeune. Commandant of the Marine Corps, 1920 to 1929 (1867 – 1942)

Major General Sir Stewart Graham Menzies. KCB, KCMG, DSA, MC. Head of the Secret Intelligence Service (1884 – 1923)

1

Near Lincheng village, Shantung Province.
0100 hours, 6 May 1923

Sun Mei-yao leans into the cool night wind, urging speed on his stallion. Three hundred cavalrymen ride with him through low hills. Most are deserters from defeated warlords who have joined Sun's bandit army because he is a skilled and formidable commander, he pays well, and he's generous when sharing loot. In return, he demands loyalty, conformity to strict military discipline, fresh uniforms, and exemplary personal hygiene.

An hour's ride away, just south of Lincheng, the rail line crosses the bridge over the Grand Canal entering Shantung Province. Sun knows that the elite Shanghai Express train must slow to a crawl so it can navigate the right-hand curve just before the canal bridge. Once clear, the train will accelerate for the gentle climb into Lincheng. It's here that Sun will make his ambush—scheduled for 0300 hours.

Earlier that day, Sun had received a coded telegram from his secret agent.

```
ALERT STOP THERE ARE TWENTY-ONE WELL-ARMED
NEPALESE GURKHAS GUARDING THE TRAIN STOP
SEVERAL OF THE OCCIDENTAL PASSENGERS APPEAR
TO BE WEALTHY AND DISPLAY A TREASURE TROVE
OF RESPLENDENT JEWELRY STOP BE CAUTIOUS STOP
DEALING WITH THE NABOB PASSENGER MANDARIN FU
KUANG—HSŰ REQUIRES SHREWD DIPLOMACY
```

Sun and his bandits reach the railroad tracks at 0200 hours. He dismounts and signals to Captain Chao Tan-keng, who splits "B" company from the main column and rides toward Lincheng. Their assignment is to neutralize the police and the Nationalist soldiers.

Sun's engineering officer, Lieutenant Yang Hasi-peng, moves his platoon to about one thousand meters north of the bridge. They begin to rip out the fishplates on one length of the right rail. When the train hits the sabotaged rail, the rail will splay to the right causing the train to derail.

"Sergeant Hsu, get those railroad torpedoes tied down on both sides of the tracks close to the bridge. I don't want that train going too fast when it derails. Dead Occidentals have no value—ransom is the big money."

Sun hears gunfire from Lincheng and, a few minutes later, a lamp flashes from the tower of the Methodist church. Chao has neutralized the threat from the town. He makes a mental note to reward his best officer.

Sun scrambles up a short incline and snaps orders. "Sergeant Tang, take your men to the high ground along the left side of the tracks and dig in. Be ready when the coach doors open." His infantrymen fan out and dig their emplacements. "Set up the machine gun on that mound—the Gurkha guards will be in the first car." Sun watches Corporal Ts'zo Banh load a belt of Mauser 8mm ammunition. While some engineers toss ripped-out fishplates into the brush, others set torpedoes on the rails. Sun's scheme is unfolding on schedule. His right flank is secure, and the Grand Canal and bridge protect his left. He surveys his ambush preparations and a feeling of great pride engulfs his soul. *How stupid of Colonel Chiang Kai-shek to dismiss me for excessive cruelty to those Communist guerillas. Crucifixion was just punishment for those Reds. First in my class at Wampoa Military Academy—the Nationalists will sorely regret rejecting me.*

The bandit commander mounts his horse to oversee the last preparations. Any moment now, he will hear the long whistle of the Shanghai Express approaching the bridge. He is ready.

2

Shanghai railroad station.
Early morning, 5 May 1923 (the previous day)

The stationmaster focuses on his pocket watch. The minute hand ticks to 0855 hours: five minutes to departure. He puts the watch in his vest, blows his whistle five times, and waves his red flag back and forth over his head. The whistle's shrill tone echoes throughout the Shanghai Railroad Station.

The fireman shovels coal into the locomotive's blazing furnace, and the engineer bleeds steam that hisses loudly and engulfs the nearby area in a white cloud. Passengers scurry to locate their cars. Handlers pull large wagons full of suitcases, boxes, mail, and other paraphernalia to the baggage car. Porters cater obsequiously to the first-class passengers, and vendors on the platform hawk a mélange of wares. At 0900 hours, the British-owned Shanghai Express train will depart for its nonstop overnight run to Peiping.

Tall and ramrod-straight Sikhs in their dastars headdress guard all the station's activities. They stand at order arms holding their British Enfield 303 rifles tight at their sides.

A squad of Gurkha soldiers stands at attention before the armored coach. Their Kashmir hats are cocked rakishly. Tucked in their belts are the traditional kukri, with eighteen-inch blades. On command from their British officer, the Nepalese guards snap their rifles to port-arms and climb aboard. Many of the British passengers pause and smile, knowing the Empire's best will be protecting them.

Swinging aboard a first-class coach is Stephan Paskhim. He carries a leather valise engraved with the double-eagle emblem of Imperial Russia. His superior intelligence radiates from black-diamond eyes.

Mahima Rahman, the tall Madras porter, asks, "May I take your case and show you to your compartment, sir?"

"No," Paskhim replies sharply and pushes past. He snaps the door shut and pulls the shade. When he opens the valise a deep frown crosses his brow.

In the passageway, Rahman brushes at the bright gold trim of his traditional shalwar kameez uniform before he raps a knuckle on the opposite door.

"Come in." Margaret Jasperson is thirty-seven and slightly over-weight. She smiles at Rahman. She wears no makeup, has no outstanding features, and yet she is comely. She has drawn her long brown hair into a tight bun. A wide-brimmed hat lies on the lamp table. A matronly purse rests on her lap.

"We will be departing soon, madam. How may I be of service?"

"I am fine, thanks."

Rahman bows and backs out, sliding the door shut.

Jasperson returns to her trip report. The American Express logo features prominently on her stationery. As the senior travel agent in the Peiping office, she arranges for Occidental businessmen, clergy, diplomats, and their staffs. She assesses the political and economic environment and evaluates safety conditions in the destination provinces.

Her eyes wander to the door. Something about the porter's unex-pected check-in does not feel right.

Unknown to her cohorts, Jasperson is a senior operative in Britain's Secret Intelligence Service, the MI6. She reports on Japanese and Soviet political, military, and diplomatic activities in China's Northern provinces, with emphasis on Manchuria and Inner Mongolia. She has a wide network of loyal Chinese and Occidental spies who collect and report information.

Just before she boarded, an aged porter had slipped her a note, sub rosa warning her that a dangerous foreign agent might be onboard.

She digs deep into her over-large purse and retrieves her Webley .455. She rotates the cylinder to confirm it is loaded and slides the safety to "Fire."

She closes her eyes, relaxes, and reviews mental images of the passengers she has seen. None stands out. Nonetheless she places the revolver within easy reach under her hat.

Rahman raps lightly on Doctor Todd Fleet's door. Hearing "Enter," he glides into the compartment of the young American missionary and his new wife, Laura.

Fleet wears a conservative gray suit with a powder-blue tie. He has bushy black hair, dark eyes, and a weak chin.

Rahman asks, "Will you be needing anything?"

Laura wears a pink flapper dress and matching cloche hat. Rahman admires the curves of her sensuous body and her exotic blond hair. Her startling hazel eyes watch him knowingly.

"How may I be of service, madam?"

"Bring me green tea, piping hot, and scones."

"Yes, madam." Rahman bows slightly. "I will begin serving in a few minutes. I have several more passengers to settle."

Miffed, she snaps, "Hurry up. I need a refresher."

Todd arches an eyebrow, amused by his new bride's imperiousness, and considers tempering this minor contretemps, but decides against it.

Rahman smiles. "As you wish, madam." He bows slightly and backs out of the compartment. He notes, *Mao Tse-tung's Eighth Route Army could use Doctor Fleet's skills. That shrew—the crocodiles for her.*

The notorious Mandarin Fu Kuang-hsű, with his two young and titillating concubines in tow, follow Rahman to their suite. The mandarin wears a traditional long black gown with thin red stripes down each side and a black skullcap with a long red tassel. His first wife, the *Qizi*, selected these two women as babies, raised the pair, and skilled them in the erotic arts. Inside, his eyes trace their classic figures, emphasized by their fetching cheongsams. His pulse skips a couple of beats as he anticipates tonight's *ménage à trois*.

The nabob Fu is a rice merchant with a monopoly spanning several provinces. He runs that part of his business anonymously, through well-paid and ruthless intermediaries. He takes a more active hand in his multinational opium trade, a string of upscale brothels in most major cities, and a chain of opium dens in the slums throughout China. He sighs and beckons the concubines to him.

Rahman pauses at the compartment of Major Quentin Ashley-Cooper, Royal Marines, DSO, and his wife, Karina. Ashley-Cooper is en route to the British embassy in Peiping as the new military *attaché*. Today he wears the tropical dress uniform. Rahman is curious about them and wonders if Ashley-Cooper or his wife could be useful. He will signal his contact, Comrade Lin Piao.

In November 1914, Ashley-Cooper led the Commonwealth troops that attacked and captured the German treaty port Tsing-tao. He took a German round in his right leg, which has forced him to use a cane—Rahman is confident that it hides a rapier.

Karina is a shy, tall, reserved woman with large hazel eyes and long dusty-brown hair. In contrast to her hard-eyed husband, she has a ready and engaging smile. She eschews the flapper style and today wears a light wool, pale blue dress—a frock that reflects taste and expense. Her father, Stanley Wilkerson, is a wealthy wool merchant who showers his only child with expensive gifts. This afternoon she is disturbed, but keeps up a brave front for the man she loves. She reflects, *I'm a soldier's wife, not a spy for the Foreign Office.*

But that's exactly what the MI6 operative at the British Consulate in Shanghai told Karina yesterday in an extensive, special-compartment intelligence briefing. He averred, "*Attaché* wives are expected to complement their husbands' intelligence gathering activities." She reluctantly signed an Official Secrets Act document.

Later that afternoon, in the consulate's basement, a Marine sergeant small-arms instructor tutored Karina in the rudiments of pistol techniques. As a loyal soldier's wife, and with misgivings, she hoisted the Webley Mark IV .38-caliber revolver, sighted the target, and fired six times in quick succession. To her instructor's amazement, she scored 39 points out of a possible 60—a respectable score. Several hours later, she consistently scored around 50.

"Congratulations, Madam Ashley-Cooper. You've done exceptionally well."

"I have no explanation. For reasons I do not understand, I am serenely at ease with this weapon in my hand."

"Best of fortune, madam."

Down the corridor is the compartment of Mister and Madam Randolph Van Halsted. He is an American multimillionaire with a railroad empire in southern Africa and a worldwide shipping line. Not satisfied with that, he is travelling to Peiping to sign a deal authorizing his rail development in northwestern China. In his money belt is a bribe for the Minister of the Interior—one hundred newly-minted $10,000 U.S. gold certificates.

Maureen is wealthy in her own right. Her father was a New York banking tycoon who left her a fortune, which she invested in Manhattan real estate. Following the advice of her young lover, a handsome electrical engineer, she purchased ten thousand shares in the newly formed Computer Tabulating Recording Company. Maureen trumpets her wealth with expensive jewelry.

Mahima Rahman proceeds along the passageway. He finds this run's passengers particularly intriguing and wonders what secrets they guard.

Mae Ling-weh, a French-Eurasian social pariah, is a striking beauty with keen intelligence. The popular rumor is that the nuns who raised her found her as a newborn baby in a trash bin. Currently, she is the successful proprietress of the upscale Panda-Bamboo restaurant in Peiping. Off the menu, but easily available, is all manner of contraband—opium paste, illicit weapons, espionage, assassination, and exotic females. Rahman notices her keen interest in the other first-class passengers and speculates as to why.

Monique Harmonie is a fading French cinema star. As she approaches forty, Monique's sex appeal still oozes off the screen. According to the tabloids, her five miscreant ex-husbands have bled her bank accounts dry. Out of desperation, she has agreed to star in a racy film set in Peiping and its environs—including some scenes on the Shanghai Express.

Rahman looks forward to viewing her new movie.

Across the hall is Nani Atticus. He is a short, husky man with bright brown eyes, a receding hairline, and a square-cut jaw. He travels with Xenia De Luca, a classic Italian beauty from Florence with large smoke-blue eyes, a Roman nose, and dark olive skin. She is a posh *fille de joie* who, with exceptional sexual skills, caters to the wealthy and well-connected. She seduced Atticus when he let slip his scheme after consuming several glasses of champagne.

Until a few months ago, Atticus was the Chief Financial Officer of Rome's Savoy Automotive. Now he is fleeing the Italian secret police, the Organization for Vigilance and Repression of Anti-Fascism (OVRA), after looting the company's treasury, abandoning his wife and three children, and stealing secret plans for a revolutionary armored tank. His money belt is stuffed with British one hundred pound sterling notes and several million dollars in United States gold certificates. His goal is Port Arthur in Manchuria, where the Japanese Kwangtung Army has promised him refuge in exchange for the Italian tank designs.

Xenia speculates that the Japanese will renege, steal his money and the plans, and then execute him. She waits.

Ensconced in the last compartment of the car is Bridget von Cairo, a sybaritic adventuress. Today, she is traveling on a Vatican passport that she blackmailed a gullible Cardinal for. She is skirting an INTERPOL arrest warrant detailing her involvement in a scheme to sell a fake *objet d'art* purported to be a rare Crusade treasure from the Knights Hospitaller of Saint John of Jerusalem and Rhodes.

The minute hand on the stationmaster's watch snaps to 0900. He waves red and white flags and blasts his whistle. Last-minute passengers rush to find their cars. Five young American flappers, laughing and jabbering, scramble aboard.

Porters slam the coach doors shut. The locomotive's bell clangs in rhythmic syncopation. The engineer releases the brakes with a howling hiss, and billowing white steam enshrouds the scene. Amongst the screeching and clamor, the locomotive's six drive-wheels spin and spit sparks, gaining purchase on the polished steel rails. Ever so slowly, the British-owned Shanghai Express inches forward for its nonstop, high-speed run to Peiping.

3

Onboard the Shanghai Express, en route to Peiping.
Cocktail Time, 5 May 1923

Around 1700 hours, the first-class passengers begin to drift into the lounge coach to imbibe before-dinner cocktails. The coach is furnished in the classic Art Deco style: strips of bright chrome adorn the edge of the bar, swirling strips of curved teak adorn the lounge chairs. Hanging on the wall are prints by Erté, Tamara de Lempicka, and Raphael Delorme. Dance music wafts from the Victrola gramophone—Ted Weem's Orchestra playing "Somebody Stole My Gal."

Todd and Laura Fleet enter hand in hand and spot Major Ashley-Cooper and Karina. Ashley-Cooper looks sharp in his mess dress uniform and Karina exudes charm in a long blue dress. Todd smiles and nods in courteous recognition.

Ashley-Cooper stands and says in acknowledgment to the couple, "Good evening."

Todd responds, "Good evening, Major." He turns to Karina. "Good evening, madam." The pair continues down the aisle.

Across the aisle, exotic Mae Ling-weh sips a tall rum drink. Her classic, bright-blue flapper dress has a short skirt that creeps ever so slowly up her thigh to proffer her long, sensuous legs, and the bodice is cut low, revealing more than it ought. It's obvious that she does not wear a *brassière*. She offers a haughty smile to the entering pair. As they pass, she follows them with her seductive eyes, appraising them. She sips her rum cocktail, and concludes quickly that they are of no import. However, he is a handsome fellow. She leans across the aisle to start a conversation with Major Ashley-Cooper and his wife about the chaos that is China. She learns that he is posted to the British Embassy in Peiping as the military *attaché*. She files this critical information in her sharp brain as a useful contact. Without doubt, she'll cultivate his friendship and more. Throughout the hour, she carefully appraises the passengers: discreetly prying into their backgrounds, assessing their wealth, appraising the value of their jewelry, and making notes about their attributes for future use. Occasionally, she flashes a short smile to Todd across the aisle.

Todd and Laura sink deep into a dark-blue settee. Todd returns Mae Ling-weh's smile, turns away, and orders a glass of Chablis for himself, and a Manhattan for Laura. Laura, not one to share her man, spouts, "That Oriental vamp is making eyes at you. Don't you dare acknowledge her."

Todd responds, "I've barely noticed her." Without thinking, his curiosity quickly overwhelms his better judgement. He raises his head, drinks in Mae's voluptuousness, and utters a barely audible grunt of approval.

With her eyes flashing, Laura jabs her elbow into Todd's rib cage. "You *roué*. She's a classic *femme fatale*. If you respond to her, your manhood will suffer—severely."

Todd wipes the guilt off his face and responds, "I may be dumb, but I'm not stupid. Cool down, and let's finish our drinks in peace." Laura stares at him with a flash of anger, tosses down her Manhattan, and orders another.

Margaret Jasperson enters and spots Todd and Laura. She walks to them, extends her hand, and smiles graciously. "Good evening, I am Margaret Jasperson. May I sit with you? I'm traveling alone and I do not know anyone on this train."

Todd stands, introduces himself and Laura, and says, "Please do, Miss Jasperson."

Seated next to Laura, Jasperson says, "Thank you. Actually, it's 'Madam.' I'm a widow. My husband, Captain Sylvester Jasperson, remains in the poppy fields of Flanders." She turns to face Laura and with a large smile says. "I appreciate your hospitality. May I offer you folks another libation?" Without waiting for an answer, she signals to Paskhim.

"Another round for this lovely couple, and a double Scotch whiskey for me, neat."

Todd completes his Chablis and faces Jasperson. "You're traveling alone?"

"Indeed. I work for American Express and my job requires that I travel frequently."

Laura takes a deep swig of her newly arrived Manhattan. "Don't you find that traveling alone is a calamity of the highest order—especially in such a remote and dangerous foreign country?"

"I'm used to it. But I do get lonely sometimes." She pauses, picks up her glass, and offers a toast to her new friends. "I'm always pleased to meet fellow travelers, especially young people." She finishes her glass. "I'm headed for Peiping, where the American Express office is located. And you folks, where are you going?"

Todd and Laura take turns explaining their upcoming adventure and their final destination, the Methodist Hospital at Ye-an in Sanshi Province.

Knowing that a cadre of Mao's Communist Eighth Route Army is bivouacked in that area, Jasperson sees an opportunity to recruit these two gullible missionaries as her unwitting agents. She mentions Mao and the Communist cadres and concludes, "Let's exchange letters often. Tell me all about your work, your life in that remote province, the general conditions in the area, and how you are getting along with that element of the Red Army that's encamped there."

Laura interrupts. "Who's Mao what's-his-name and what Red Army? I've not heard about this stuff."

Japserson responds, "My dear, it's a long and bitter history. Suffice it to say, the Reds' long-term goal is to make China a Communist state— much as in that horrid Soviet Union. I reckon that eventually they will succeed, just as the Bolsheviks conquered Imperial Russia. Nowadays, the Communists are consolidating power by garnering the respect and loyalty of the peasants. But, not to worry. As Occidentals, and especially as Americans, you'll see that they will make every effort to engender your goodwill." She sips her second round of Scotch, and smiles innocently. "Do, dears, please keep me informed. I've grown fond of you already. Your information might save me a trip there. I'd be ever so grateful."

Sitting across the aisle from Major Ashley-Cooper and Karina are Randolph Van Halsted and his wife, Maureen. They project a grandiose attitude as each sips a gin rickey cocktail. Maureen gossips incessantly about the females in her social circle, focusing especially on their extramarital affairs, and makes snide comments about her fellow passengers. Tonight, she wears an *éclat* of expensive jewelry. Randolph pays faux attention to her babblings and wonders when the secret cancer in his lungs will force him into an underground compound with daisies on top. Can his son carry on? He should have brought him instead of Maureen. But she insisted.

Monique Harmonie sashays into the lounge car. Her dress is *outré*. She has eschewed a *brassière* and her gossamer thin, flaming-red dress is cut far too low for propriety. She gives a hearty wave to all and greets them with a big cinema smile and a sexy, "*Bonsoir, bon amis. Je suis Monique Harmonie dês Paris.*" Several of the male passengers gasp in pleasurable astonishment at her shocking display and nod in return recognition. Only Major Ashley-Cooper rises in respect. Most of the Occidental females are shocked with embarrassment and avert their eyes. Karina understands the dynamics of the scene and smiles politely at her.

Maureen Van Halsted wonders how any female could be so brazen nowadays, even in this permissive jazz age. Maureen whispers into her husband's ear and he raises his eyebrows and takes a furtive look at Monique. With a deep frown, he returns his gaze to Maureen, takes his wife's hand, and pats it softly. "Definitely not our type," he whispers. He returns to his cocktail and a faint smile creeps over his hard face as he recalls some of the assignations he's had with nubile young women seeking his patronage. The image of the enchanting and brazen Emmanuelle floods his mind. Never has he had such intense erotic pleasure. Their trysts were in his suite at the

Le Royal Monceau Hotel on the *Champs Elysees* last spring—*or was it two springs ago,* he tries to recall. *It's difficult with all these assignations.*

Realizing that she has had a cold reception, Monique scans the passengers. Not seeing a single man, she chooses an unoccupied lounge chair next to Major Ashley-Cooper. In only slightly accented English she comments, "Thank you, Major, for your courtesy. The rest of these egalitarian stuffed shirts do not recognize my cinematic art." She withdraws a light shawl from her purse and wraps it around her shoulders, effectively covering her bosom. She introduces herself and shakes Ashley-Cooper's hand. His wife, Karina, no prude, smiles faintly and welcomes Monique to chat with them.

Mae Ling-weh, ensconced across the aisle, appraises the cinema actress and concludes that Monique is a *tete folle*—a scatterbrain and not much more than an expensive whore. Nonetheless, whores can be useful.

Stephan Paskhim, with his valise tucked under his arm, stops just inside the entrance and keenly surveys the scene. He spots Jasperson, chooses a lounge chair across the aisle from her, and slips the valise between his hip and the arm of the chair.

Sitting next to Paskhim is Bridget von Cairo. She is an astute observer of the human condition—her stock in trade and source of her livelihood. Her red and black flapper dress is conservative, but it hints of her provoking female body. Bridget has taken the measure of all those in the coach and has concerns that all is not what it seems to be. However, she likes what she sees in Paskhim, the only single man in the coach, and she is intrigued by what is in that valise that he protects so assiduously. Bridget, in desperate need of a protector, reckons that this fellow could well be her passport to evading the pursuing INTERPOL agents. She tries to engage Paskhim in conversation, but he does not seem interested. She hails Rahman and orders a bottle of Dom Perignon champagne and two flutes. When Rahman serves her wine, she leans toward Paskhim, smiles, and makes sure that her breasts brush against his shoulder. "Join me with this fine wine." Without waiting for his answer, she thrusts the flute towards him. "Come now, let's be friendly. It's my treat."

Paskhim cocks one eyebrow and turns his head toward Cairo. He carefully peruses the woman and concludes that such an intriguing female could be useful—besides, it has been a while since he has been with an Occidental woman. He cracks his wooden face into a forced smile. "*Mademoiselle*, I am pleased to join you." He accepts the flute, tips it in salute to her, and exclaims, "*Vashe zrodovye*." He takes a small sip, smiles, and says, "Excellent. Please excuse my brutish behavior earlier. I was deep in thought about the meeting I'll have in Peiping."

The pair finishes this bottle of the bubbly and begins another. They engage in perfunctory badinage. Knowing that she has sealed the pact, Bridget whispers, "I sense trouble brewing on this train. Conspiracies are permeating the atmosphere in this coach."

Paskhim takes her arm and with eyes narrowed, he dissembles.

"Interesting that you should notice this, I do also. Perhaps it is best if we remain close."

Unobtrusively, Jasperson has monitored the *tête-à-tête* across the aisle. She wonders if Bridget is an agent—a *femme fatale* as it were. And without a doubt, Paskhim is a rogue who bears close watching.

The coeds, Mindy, Bertie, Thea, Bonny, and Melinda, dressed in unseemly flapper dresses, frolic into the lounge singing "Let's Misbehave" to a Charleston jazz beat. The silence and disparaging stares that greet their loud intrusion communicate to the students that they should cease, and behave—this lounge car is not a speakeasy on Eighth Avenue. Perfectly chastised, they find empty chairs, order alcoholic drinks, mostly gin concoctions, and either remain silent or speak to their partners in whispers. Soon the hubbub of passengers talking, laughing, and flirting returns to full volume.

Suddenly, a hush imbues the lounge coach as Fu Kuang-hsǔ and his two comely concubines enter. He is in a scarlet-red changshan with gold vest, and the two women wear the classic tight-fitting cheongsam that enhances their abundant sensuous curves. These dresses are slit to their upper thighs, exposing beautifully curved long legs. Fu bows deeply to the passengers on each side of the coach. With his shoulders square, Fu strolls down the aisle with his *demimondes* close behind. The eroticism of flashing, luscious female legs and sensuous *derrières* swinging in erotic syncopation mesmerizes the male passengers. The Occidental women avert their eyes and vow to speak harshly to their male companions.

Fu spots a settee close to the rear door that leads to a small observation platform. He orders oolong tea and scones. In the presence of elite Occidentals, his women cast their eyes down, cross their ankles, and remain mute. Their embarrassment is obvious. Once settled, Fu seems to pay the passengers no notice. Actually, with his keen human assessment skills, he takes the measure of all in the coach and senses trouble is afoot, but from whom and when, he cannot discern. Nonetheless, a thin smile crosses his lips as he anticipates the erotic pleasures awaiting him after dinner in a free-flowing *ménage à trois*.

On another settee, across the aisle from Fu, are Nani Atticus and his beautiful traveling companion Xenia De Luca. They have ignored the developing scene in the lounge coach—content to sip their Sauvignon Blanc and chat about their future under Japanese protection in Manchuria— free from the pursuing OVRA. Nani wears a finely cut, black-tie evening suit. Xenia sparkles in a light blue, red trimmed, short flapper dress that obliquely hints at her luscious body.

Atticus is deeply enamored of the gorgeous Xenia. Although she does not return his affection with sincerity, she has skillfully ensnared Atticus with her easy mien, sharp mind, beguiling flattery, and unbridled sex. She has no intention of living with this middle-aged thief under the Japanese aegis and in one of the remotest places on the planet. Her objective is that fat money belt around his waist. Her scheme is unfolding according to plan.

At 1800 hours exactly, Mahima Rahman enters the lounge coach with his Deagan four-toned xylophone chime cradled in his left arm. Wielding the mallet with deft skills, he plays the "Call to Dinner." Arriving almost on cue, this timely *deus ex machina* eases the tension suffusing throughout the room, and the passengers begin to move to the dining coach.

4

First-Class Compartments, Shanghai Express.
2100 hours, 5 May 1923

Satiated, most of the diners return to the club car, some pairing with their dinner companions to continue a newfound fellowship. Rahman is behind the bar with an array of liqueur bottles. The men crowd the bar with orders.

To the rear of the club car, Mae Ling-weh and Randolph Van Halsted engage in quiet conversation. Maureen has no interest in their chatter and excludes herself from their conversation. She retrieves a magazine. Finding it of no interest, she tosses it on the table and resigns herself to another boring evening. She tells her husband, "It's late and I'm tired. I'm going to our compartment. Be quiet when you enter."

Almost automatically, Van Halsted responds, "Yes, dear."

During dinner, Mae had finessed several hints from Van Halsted about his mission.

With subtle encouragement, faux interest, and several bottles of champagne, he has said more than he ought. Mae has resolved to ferret out all the particulars—especially the pay-off details.

"That's interesting, Mister Van Halsted. Please continue." She flashes her long right leg as she moves to retrieve a package of cigarettes from the side table. She leans close to him, smiles coyly, and purrs, "A light, please."

Van Halsted complies. No fool, he rises and says, "Excuse me, please. I need to attend to my wife. Good evening."

Nani Atticus and Xenia De Luca stroll to the club car for an after-dinner cordial. She has her right arm around his waist and whispers in his ear. A coy smile creeps across his face as he goes to the bar. She retreats to a lounge chair and applies rouge to her cheeks.

They don't stay long.

Major Ashley-Cooper and Karina enter with Monique Harmonie, their dinner companion.

Harmonie turns and, with excessive animation, proclaims slightly too loudly, "*Mes amis*," as she moves toward the bar. "*Avec plaisir, s'il vous plaît.*" The men crowding the bar give way for the effusive cinema actress.

Bridget von Cairo stands behind the crowd. She spots Stephan Paskhim. Unfortunately, Rahman did not seat them at the same table. Accordingly, she did not have the opportunity to set her hook, as it were. *It's time for me to vamp this Russian.* She fakes being pushed into Paskhim, and ensures that both her breasts rub against his back. "Excuse me, Stephan."

He swings about, sees her, and mutters, "*Mademoiselle* Bridget. How nice to see you." He takes her hand and asks, "What may I order for you?"

"My apologies. I was pushed." In her most "come hither" voice, von Cairo purrs, "Please, sir, order an ouzo for me. It's impossible for me to get to the bar."

"An ouzo?" He pauses for a second. "An anisette?"

"If you please, *monsieur*."

"Very well." Shortly, he hands her the ouzo.

"*Merci, Monsieur.*" She takes a sip. "How very kind. Please, let us sit and chat and continue our before-dinner conversation. You intrigue me." She flashes her most seductive smile and sips her ouzo. "Perhaps we can discover a personal interest to our mutual benefit."

Standing in place, Paskhim takes Cairo's arm, turns her to face him, and pulls her close to him. "Mistress von Cairo. You are an enchanting and desirable woman, but why consort with me?" His eyes narrow. "I am an indigent White Russian of no particular artistic achievement, or countenance, or financial heft."

"Perhaps, *monsieur,* it matters not." She wiggles out of his grip, deeply sips her ouzo, and rivets her deep purple eyes on his. "Very well. If I must." She straightens her shoulders and says firmly, "You are the only single man in this section of the train and I tagged you as an adventurous soul." She pauses to gain strength. "I need a patron. I'm in serious trouble."

"Trouble? What sort of trouble?"

"The police. INTERPOL is after me."

Paskhim pushes her slightly away from him. "INTERPOL trouble I do not need." He affirms his statement with authority. "Perhaps we ought to call it a night and go on our own ways."

Von Cairo smiles seductively. "I can make it worth your while. I have a quite large stash of Swiss francs hidden in Macao. And I'm here on this train."

Paskhim puts his arms akimbo and stares at her with his hard eyes. Several seconds later, he turns to the bar and takes his Chartreuse. "What manner of trouble?"

"Nothing really. A misunderstanding. Actually, of no import." She fumbles in her purse for a cigarette, lights it, and inhales deeply. Her ruby-red lips form a perfect oval and she exhales slowly. The smoke drifts upward in a lazy spiral.

Becoming agitated at her selective dawdling, he demands, "Do not take me for a fool. An INTERPOL arrest warrant is serious business. Tell me!"

With a flourish, she takes another deep drag, the released smoke enveloping her response. "Very well, if you insist." *That Russian bastard. I'll get his valise, no matter what.* "I'm wanted on a charge of fraud. It is alleged that I swindled a renowned collector with a fake *objet d'art.* Actually, this so-called collector is a notorious international gangster, and he's lying, of course."

Paskhim tries to suppress a small laugh. "Of course."

Mindy and the other college girls, slightly tipsy from the free-flowing champagne at dinner, gambol into the club car doing their version of a buck-and-wing dance routine. Bertie slips a record on the gramophone: it's the Jimmy Lunceford Band playing "Varsity Drag." The girls go into a rousing Charleston routine and dance up and down the aisle. Thea grabs Todd Fleet for her partner and swings him into the dance. He engages the beautiful and top-heavy sans-brassiere Thea with gusto, and displays surprising terpsichorean skills. At the conclusion of the record, the dancers make a bow, and the passengers applaud vigorously. Another jazz tune blares from the gramophone—it's going to be a long, noisy night.

Monique Harmonie joins the college students in various jazz dances. Even the men blush.

Seeing that Monique has joined the dancers, Quentin Ashley-Cooper and Karina rise, wave to Monique, and retire to their compartment.

Todd Fleet is mesmerized by Monique's erotic dance. Laura is embarrassed and her eyes flash fury. Abruptly, she slaps him, shouts, "Libertine!" and takes French leave.

Paskhim frowns deeply in disapproval and says, "Let's adjourn to my compartment where it's quiet. I can't stand this American jazz and these passengers' incessant and inane jabbering. The noise level is intolerable."

Bridget smiles coyly. "You are a rascal. Let's go."

地陽

Jasperson enters her compartment and locks it. She frowns as she slides into the lounge chair and covers her legs with a light blanket. She's inexplicably apprehensive. From long experience, she has sensed that something, she cannot tell what, is deeply troubling her. She reviews the evening and cannot recall anything that she said or did that would engender such concern. *I'm certain that I did not, no matter how slight, do or say anything untoward that might compromise my mission or cover. Yet, this disquiet infects my soul. What the hell is it?* She rises, retrieves her Webley revolver, and slips it under the blanket.

Jasperson opens her traveling flask and takes a deep, quick swig of Scotch whiskey. The smooth liquid strolls down her throat. Shortly after, the frown fades and a slow smile sneaks across her face. *That's better. So what if there is a "dangerous" foreign agent onboard—as my agent said?* Her eyes narrow. *What's that to do with me? Perhaps nothing, I reckon.* She eyes the flask and concludes, *once again.* She hoists the flask to her lips and drains it. *Damn! That's good.* Soon, her concerns fade away and she relaxes. On impulse, she caresses the flask with deliberate care, and holds it at arm's length. Fading in on the flask's chrome are faux images of her young and loving husband in the trenches during the carnage at Flanders. He scrambles out of the trench and goes over the top. His image fades. She cries, "Shelly!" The words of Lieutenant Colonel John McCrae's poem flash into her mind. Unselfconsciously she whispers, "In Flanders fields the poppies blow between the crosses, row on row." Soft tears trickle down her cheeks as she continues, "Loved and were loved, and now we lie, in Flanders fields." *Which cross bears my Sylvester's name?* A flood of tears rushes down her cheeks. *I love you, Shelly, so deeply. God, I miss you.* Trying to recover, she wipes her tears with the sleeve of her gown. *I'm getting maudlin.* She checks the flask. It's empty. *My love is gone, and that was long ago.* With building resolve, she sits upright in the lounge chair, her eyes narrow, and she affirms, *Now I serve King and Country with all my being.*

She closes her eyes and reviews the developing scene. She nods, and slips into a light sleep.

池 呃 匽

Paskhim silently closes his compartment door and locks it.

Van Cairo asks, "What have you to drink?"

"Nothing in here. Shall I go to the bar?"

"Not necessary. Let's continue our talk."

"Not necessary."

池 呃 匽

Paskhim slips on his robe and looks at the sleeping von Cairo for several seconds. He stoops and carefully pulls away a lock that has fallen over her right eye. *Indeed, you are a beautiful woman and deftly skilled in carnality.*

He carefully lifts her head, strips the sash from his robe, and loops it around her neck. "Strumpet!" He tightens the *garrotte* slowly.

Von Cairo awakens, her eyes pulsing with fear. Her hands reflexively grasp the unyielding *garrotte*, but cannot overcome its ever-tightening grip. Her eyes plead for mercy.

Paskhim continues to tighten the sash. "No, no, my dear. You are a liability. I do not need you. Nonetheless, be assured that I will filch your stash in Macao—if any." He continues to increase the pressure. "You were a reckless fool to give me the details. Should I communicate your demise to INTERPOL?" He makes a short, snorting laugh at his joke.

Von Cairo's hands fall away and her fearful eyes stare lifelessly at the ceiling. Paskhim lowers her head to the pillow. He strips away his sash and loops it around his robe.

In a demented *volte-face*, he continues his conversation with the dead. "You bumbling-face idiot. I know that you are—excuse me, were, a free-lance agent working for the Chinese Nationalists' Investigation and Statistics Bureau. Now, we might say, that the secrets in my valise are safe, *nest-ce pas, mon cher.*" He retreats to a chair, sits, and puts his right hand to his face. *Will the Japanese pay me a bonus for eliminating this Chinese intelligence agent? I will ask.*

The adrenaline drains away and Paskhim relaxes. He surveys the murder scene and wonders if he has gone too far. *In a way, that bitch had possibilities. After I had tamed her, she would have made a welcome traveling companion—for a while.*

Resigned, he slowly climbs out of the chair, opens the window over the bed, lifts the dead woman, and tosses her out the window. "*Adieu, mon amour.*"

池�

Tired from the frenetic dancing, Monique Harmonie returns to her compartment, retrieves a bottle of Château de Montifaud Cognac, and collapses into the lounge chair. *At last.* With deft skill, she removes the gold foil, extracts the cork, sniffs the pleasant aroma, and takes a deep swig directly from the bottle. *To hell with convention. I'm thirsty.* A pleasant glow suffuses through her mind and body; she begins to relax, and slides deeper and deeper into the comfortable chair. Several minutes later, she twitches upright, fully alert. *Very well. I'm ready.* She begins to review her upcoming task. She ties her hair into a bun and pins it, slips into a sheer, white peignoir sans *brassiere* and dainties, applies faint rouge to her cheeks, ties a blue ribbon at her throat, and dons blue slippers. She checks the effect in the mirror. Satisfied, she exits her compartment, moves to Paskhim's door, and knocks softly.

Paskhim is making his evening toilet. Surprised at a knock this late at night, he utters, "What the hell! Damn." *Could it be related to this evening's irregular activities here? No. Not possible.* Seriously annoyed, he ambles to the door. "Who are you? What do you want?"

In a soft voice she says, "I am Monique Harmonie. I have a message for you."

"What message? From whom?"

"Not in the hall, *monsieur. S'il vous plaît.*"

Now he is curious at such a late-night meeting, and cautious because he knows no one on the train, especially that sexy French actress. He fetches his Lugar pistol. "Stand back." He cracks the door slightly and sees Harmonie dressed for an assignation. More curious than alarmed at the scene, he wonders, *what now?* He opens the door. "Come in."

"*Bonsoir, monsieur.* I received this message from a well-dressed Japanese person at the Shanghai Station. I am to deliver it to you sub rosa. He sends his apologies for having missed you."

"Japanese. Sub rosa? I am at a loss to understand. What message? Why are you carrying a message for me?"

"British pounds sterling, *monsieur.* Genuine coin of the realm, as it were." She smiles mischievously at her fib.

Not understanding, he demands, "Give that message to me and go away." Distracted by her revealing ensemble, he can't stop gazing at her femininity, and wonders where she has the message stashed.

"Of course." With swift motion, she pulls the pin from her hair bun, twirls, and jams it deep into Paskhim's left eye. Her action was so swift that all he saw was a winged blur.

He screams from the searing pain, drops the Lugar, and falls back. Harmonie rushes in, cuts him with a karate chop to the neck, and kicks him in the crotch with her steel reinforced slipper. He tumbles back toward the bed. His right eye is wide with pain and fear. He cannot scream with his throat crushed. She closes the door quietly. "Paskhim, you have curare circulating in your blood towards your heart. You are of the deceased. Soon paralysis will spread throughout your body. In a few minutes, you'll expire due to asphyxiation. *Adieu.*"

She spots the valise that he has assiduously guarded, snaps the lock, opens it, removes the papers, and quickly scans them. She cries aloud, "*Mon Dieu!* It cannot be!" Her eyes open wide, her mouth shuts tight. A deep frown digs into her forehead. She tosses the papers on Paskhim's body. "You win. Bastard!" She enjoins, "*Va au diable.*" She stares at the front page of *The Shanghai Times* newspaper—it now covers the dead man's face. On the floor is the menu from a Russian restaurant. *Merde!*

5

Monique Harmonie's Compartment, Shanghai Express.
2230 hours, 5–6 May 1923

Chagrined at her debacle, having failed to recover the Japanese plans for guerrilla-inspired activities in French Indo-China, Harmonie checks the hall to see if it is clear and makes a hasty retreat to her compartment. She jams the lock home and double-checks to ensure it's tight.

Paskhim's scream had penetrated Jasperson's door. When she put her ear to the door, she heard nothing. She slipped back into her lounge chair—her mind whirled. *That must have been Paskhim. I wonder. No doubt he's met with foul play. The question is, who caused him such pain? Is he dead? To what end? Now, that quiet from across the hall bodes ill.* Reflexively, she grabs tight her Webley 455, screws on a silencer, and twirls the cylinder—all rounds are in place. Soon, she relaxes her grip and replaces the weapon under the blanket covering her knees. *I reckon there is more skullduggery afoot tonight, and I do not know who the players are. Who are the knights and who are the blackguards?* Alert, she eschews sleep and rings for Rahman to bring tea to help keep her awake. Not long after, she is sipping the deep-brown liquid and luxuriating in its pleasant aroma and taste.

Harmonie falls into the lounge chair and breathes deeply to slow her heartbeat. She grabs the cognac and swigs deeply. The calming effect is quick. *Damn! Assassination is not my forte—that Russian was only my second kill. My specialty is the* fille de joie—*a part I excel in.* She swigs again and a pleasant glow envelops her body and mind. She smiles broadly and reflects on her past successful assignations as an agent for the *Deuxième Bureau*. She scoots her *derrière* further down in the chair. *The Bureau's trainers taught me well in the martial arts and in the erotic arts—skills that were beyond my comprehension as a schoolgirl in the convent of The Sisters of Mary Magdalene in Hanoi.* She laughs quietly at the contradiction. *If Mother Superior, Sister Elizabeth Margaret, could see me now, she would be scandalized and would rap my knuckles with her ever-present ruler.* She closes her eyes as the cognac takes control of her. Within a few minutes, she leaps out of her chair. *Dieu Merci! How do I explain my mischance to my controller in Haiphong? She will be most disappointed. Nonetheless, her instructions were clear. The Bureau was convinced that Paskhim was a courier for Japan's Black Dragon Society and that he had those documents.* Another swig of cognac sets her mind at ease. *C'est la vie.*

Realizing that she must have assistance to get rid of the Russian's body, she changes into a conservative dress and shoes. *Whom can I trust? No matter who it is, I will expose my cover.* While completing her ensemble, she reflects on her childhood in Dà Nàng as a French *colon: the daughter of a successful rubber planter, a convent girl, my Legionnaire brother, Laurent, dead at the siege of German Treaty Port Tsingtao in 1914. My parents killed and their plantation destroyed by Japanese-influenced nationalist guerillas.* Kindled anew is her anger at the enemies of France that destroyed her young life. She resolves, *I am a citizen of the Third Republic—and proud to serve Marianne.*

She considers asking Margaret Jasperson for help. However, on reflection, she disregards this idea. *No. No indeed. No passengers. Too risky.* Flummoxed, she slumps in the chair. *Who? Leave Paskhim's body in his room? Not a feasible idea. It would be the British police investigating the Russian's murder. The hairpin clue would clearly point to a woman. I do not relish spending my life in a Chinese prison.* Another swig of cognac energizes her thinking. *Rahman, the steward. Perhaps. He seems to be a man of the world who would be receptive to a little knavery, given a sufficient bribe.* She rings for him.

Rahman arrives promptly and knocks.

Harmonie calls, *"Entrer."*

Rahman opens her door. At this late hour, he asks in an annoyed voice, "How may I be of service, *mademoiselle?*"

Harmonie appraises him and concludes that he might do. "Come in, Rahman. I wish to speak with you."

In his most formal voice, he replies, "Sorry, Mistress Harmonie, it is forbidden for me to fraternize with the passengers. May I bring you tea? A glass of champagne, perhaps?"

Her eyes frown at his reticence, and in a sharp voice she orders, "No. Nothing. Come in and close the door. I have a simple task for you that will pay handsomely."

Not one to skip a paying proposition, he ignores her disparaging mien. He responds politely, "As you ask, *mademoiselle*" With some trepidation, he enters and stands next to the open door.

"Close the door and lock it."

Now with serious disquiet, Rahman answers, "No, *mademoiselle*. Please speak forthrightly. What have you for me? Else I must return to my station."

With a coquettish smile, Harmonie purrs, "I want you to get rid of Paskhim's body."

Taken aback at such an outlandish request, and with questioning eyes, he fumbles, "Surely, you jest?"

"Indeed not. He is in the compartment across the hall. Do it, and twenty-five thousand French francs are yours."

"I must return to my station. Good evening, Mistress Harmonie."

"Would thirty-five thousand francs tempt you?"

Sensing that she is serious, he asks, "How, may I inquire, did Mister Paskhim come to such an end?"

"It's simple enough, I killed him."

Shocked, he recovers his thoughts and asks, "Would I be indelicate if I were to ask why you performed such a deed?"

With a lace hanky she dabs faux tears. With imploring eyes, she says shyly, "He lured me into his compartment on a false premise and made improper advances. Even though I pleaded with him to stop, he would not. For some reason, he was convinced that I was a woman of easy virtue—a *demimonde*, as it were."

"Mister Paskhim was a well-built man. I wonder how you accomplished such a homicide."

With a smug smile of accomplishment, she replies, "I kicked him in the groin, and jabbed my hairpin into his brain through his eye." She tosses the hanky on the bed, and demands, "Convinced?"

Rahman places his arms akimbo. "Perhaps, *mademoiselle*." Turning toward the door, he says, "I should like to see the body. If you do not mind."

Energized that she now has his attention, she cracks open her door and leads him into Paskhim's room. She nods her head slightly toward the bed. "There he is."

Rahman goes to the bed, inspects the pin in Paskhim's eye, and to make sure, he takes the Russian's pulse. Assured, he says, "Congratulations, you've done mankind a service. This Russian was an evil man."

"Enough. Lift him. I will lead the way to the platform outside the lounge car. Toss him over."

"Not yet, *mademoiselle*. I must see the color of your money."

"I do not carry such large sums with me. In these chaotic times, it would be foolhardy. On arrival in Peiping tomorrow, I will take you to the *Banque de L'Indo Chino* and give you the payment. Satisfactory?"

"No."

"What then?" She reflects that her carefully constructed scheme may be collapsing. With a hint of desperation in her voice, she asks, "Would you accept a down payment?"

"Perhaps. What do you propose?"

"Me. You can have me tonight," she responds with a dispassionate voice and face.

Rahman cocks his head and stares at the French woman with his hard dark eyes. *Only an Occidental would make such a sordid bargain. Since, on orders from Red counterintelligence officials, I was going to murder Paskhim myself, I might as well accept—there is nothing to lose and lots to gain. And I will have the option to blackmail this lewd woman.* "Very well, I agree."

A few minutes later, the pair stands on the outdoor platform behind the lounge car. Rahman opens the iron picket gate and tosses the Russian's body off the train. Before he can turn around, Harmonie gives him a vicious karate chop to the base of his neck and kicks him in the back. He tumbles into the night. With deliberate precision, she closes the gate and secures its lock.

On the adrenaline-induced high, she is proud of herself for executing a successful coup. She gives a salute to the deceased Rahman and says, "*Au revoir, mon ami.*" As the stimulating drug begins to drain, and the narcotic effect of false courage from the cognac wanes, doubts creep into her soul. Anxiety engulfs her, and she perspires profusely. For a long time, with both hands tightly gripping the railing, she stares into the night as if to ensure that the steward truly is dead.

As she slowly walks toward her compartment, the enormity of her dual murders this evening challenges what minute morality remains from the convent sisters' cultivation of her soul. "Mon Dieu! *I have no heart for* meurtre. *I am a prostitute*—une pute! *That's what I am.*" Her heart begins to race irregularly. She continues her doleful walk, and is thankful that the hall is abandoned. She stops at Jasperson's door. *I need to talk to her—an older woman will understand this disquietude I suffer.* She knocks softly.

Instantly alert, Jasperson rises and puts her Webley at the ready. "Yes?"

"I am Monique Harmonie. May I speak with you, please?"

"It's almost three o'clock—far too late for chit chat. We'll talk in the morning."

"Please, *madame*. It is important. Perhaps you can help me."

Sensing that the reason for the unease she's experienced most of this evening is at her door, she inquires, "What is so important? And how may I be of help?"

Exasperated at the delay, Harmonie says in a quiet voice, "I must confess my sins this evening to someone who would understand."

Jasperson cracks her door open slightly and sees the distressed Harmonie. Anxious to know what the "sins" are, she opens the door and says, "Come in, Monique, quickly."

Harmonie enters, collapses into the lounge chair, and begins to sob uncontrollably. Through her tears she mutters, *"Merci, madame."*

Jasperson locks her door. She turns away from the sobbing woman, lifts her skirt, and jams the Webley into a holster strapped to her left inner thigh. With the weapon secured, she pours a stiff Scotch whiskey. "Drink this," she commands.

Without comment, Harmonie sips the brown liquid, and places her head at the back of the lounge chair.

"Use this hanky to wipe your tears and blow your nose."

With those tasks accomplished, except for Harmonie's quiet tears, silence infuses the compartment. Eventually, Jasperson says, "Better, Monique?"

Harmonie nods her head in the affirmative.

"Very well. Let's talk. What sins are causing you such distress?"

With her eyes wide, she exclaims, "Murder! Two murders. I committed two murders this evening." She drinks deep from the glass of Scotch.

Unsure what to make of this startling admission, Jasperson calmly asks. "Whom did you murder, cinema actress?"

With stilted emotion, Harmonie responds, "The Russian, Paskhim and the steward, Rahman."

Sensing that she is close to the explanation for Paskhim's scream, Jasperson, asks with faux motherly affection, "Monique, murder is such a heinous deed. Pray tell, why would you slay these two fellows?"

Gaining courage, she drains the glass. Now on a first-name basis, Harmonie responds, "Margaret, it is a complicated story. Suffice it to say that both were evil men and deserved their fates." She uses the hanky to wipe a lingering tear. "Please understand, *madame*, that I am not a paid assassin, but occasionally I am compelled to eliminate rogues."

Jasperson stares at the actress. Shortly, she asks in her most empathetic voice, "If I may be impertinent, how do you accomplish such tasks?"

Woozy from the Scotch and feeling much better, Harmonie speaks with a slightly slurred voice. "With martial arts and curare. The instructors at the *Deuxième Bureau* taught me well." Instantly she gasps, and throws her right hand to her mouth at her outrageous *faux pas*.

Curare! From French Guiana, no doubt. Yes, that certainly would be the French tactic. "An agent for French Intelligence? Well done, Monique. Show me your credentials," demands Jasperson.

"No. I do not have them. It would be suicide for me to carry such documents."

To advance quickly the unfolding scene, Jasperson says, "All right. I believe you." Jasperson refills Harmonie's glass and fixes one for herself. "Tell me about your operations."

Keenly aware of her miscue and stung by Jasperson's inopportune demand, Harmonie says forcefully, "*Non.* You have no right to ask such a confidential question. I refuse."

"I know who you work for, and that you are a murderess. Cooperate with me. I'm a reasonable person. I would help you. In fact, I may have some opportunities for a woman of your talents. My pay is excellent."

Shocked that her newfound friend would want to hire her for espionage tasks, Harmonie exclaims, "*Madame*, I suspect that you are more than you pretend. *N'est-ce pas?*"

"Perhaps. Travel agents in this part of the world must move cautiously and have access to many services." Jasperson swigs the liquor, smiles broadly, and promises, "I will keep your secrets."

Resigned that she has no reasonable option against the subtly suggested blackmail, Harmonie begins, "I have the near-perfect cover—a promiscuous, not too bright, fading cinema actress. I travel worldwide, and meet and socialize with the highest echelons of society: tycoons, heads of state, bankers, diplomats, and high-ranking military officers. How easy I find it to collect information in quiet pillow-talk and to purloin classified documents from unlocked *attaché* cases."

"As I suspected. Frankly, Monique, you are too much into your cover. I would suggest that you tone it down." Jasperson picks up her Scotch.

"Drink up, Monique Harmonie, to better times." Both salute each other with raised glasses and take deep swigs. Jasperson continues, "Do you have a gun, Harmonie?"

"*Mais bien sûr.* I have a Brevete 6.35 semi-automatic. It is a small thing that I keep in a secret compartment in my toilet kit. The instructor at the *Bureau's* range says I am an excellent shot, *à la perfection.*"

Jasperson suggests, "You'd best get it and the spare clips. Spend the night in here. I suspect there's more chicanery due tonight, or should I say this morning. We'll do better as a team than as two singles."

"Excellent suggestion. I'll return shortly with my pistol and some cognac." Harmonie smiles, goes to the door, and grasps the handle.

Jasperson, quick as a diamondback strike, draws her Webley and fires. Harmonie crashes into the door and slips to the floor. There's a rather large hole oozing blood in the back of her head. "Lorelei! Paskhim was my sleeper agent deep inside Japan's Black Dragon Society."

6

First-Class Compartment, Shanghai Express.
Earlier that evening, 5–6 May 1923

Todd and Laura are asleep in each other's arms. Marital love quickly healed their contretemps.

Quentin Ashley-Cooper and Karina eschew sleep to talk about his new assignment as the military *attaché* in Peiping. Earlier, Rahman had brought a pot of coffee and a matching pair of Ming-blue cups and saucers. They sip the tasty black liquid and chat quietly.

Karina again voices her concern. "I don't like those damn guns, and I don't want to be a spy for the Crown."

Quentin tries to calm Karina's unease. "Sweetheart, you're not a spy. Spies are people that we recruit to work for us. Technically, we are 'agents' and it's our duty to collect intelligence from spies, and others who have valuable information. As with any military *attaché*, it's no secret that we're intelligence agents with diplomatic cover." He pats her on the knee and says, "It will be the rare occasion when we would need to use our guns in self-defense." Ashley-Cooper reminds her of her outstanding score on the firing range. "Karina, get your Webley .38 and let's review firing positions, safety procedures, and cleaning techniques. I'll fetch mine and we'll exchange information."

Fu Kuang-hsü, completely exhausted, is sprawled on his bed and snores loudly. Soft giggles waft throughout the compartment. His two concubines explore various erotic techniques—those that the *Qizi* proffered from the back of the book.

Secured in her compartment, Mae Ling-weh smiles broadly at her successful evening and continues to write in her diary. She records every important detail she has gleaned from the passengers. Critical information for future operations.

Nani Atticus is fast asleep after an exhilarating carnal session with Xenia De Luca's unbridled enthusiasm. Xenia has decided, *I can't waste anymore time. Tomorrow afternoon is Peiping. Nani will meet his Japanese contact at the station, and from that time on we will be under the protection of the Black Dragon Society—there will be no escape. I'll not spend the rest of my life in remote and inhospitable Manchuria. Perchance, were an opportunity to flee, the Japanese would ensure that the OVRA would have me in one of their torture chambers in no time.* She changes into comfortable clothes—a knee-length skirt, long-sleeve blouse, a light coat, and walking shoes. She looks at Nani. *That traitor is out for the evening.* She takes Nani's money belt off the bed table, removes the ten United States $10,000 gold certificates and two hundred, British £100 notes, and slips them into Nani's valise. She checks her watch: it's 0253 hours. The train begins to slow as it approaches the Grand Canal Bridge. With his valise in hand, she opens the compartment door, looks at Nani, gives him a snappy salute, and says, *"Buona notte, il mio amonte."* She disappears down the hall, towards the lounge car. Now the train is moving at its slowest pace. She grabs a bottle of Napoleon brandy, opens the lounge's rear door, moves to the platform, drops off, and fades into the night.

Next door to Margaret Jasperson are Randolph and Maureen Van Halsted. The sound of the Webley's muffled shot rouses the dozing Randolph. He awakens his wife and exclaims, "That sounds like a gunshot from Jasperson's compartment. There's chaos brewing. Get up, Maureen." With nothing more said, both roll out of bed and dress quickly.

Maureen opens her purse and withdraws a small Beretta 32. She deftly drops the magazine and sees that all cartridges are in place. She jams the magazine home with the heel of her right hand, snaps the receiver back, and releases it to advance a cartridge into the chamber. "It's not much, but better than nothing." She sticks the Beretta in her belt. "That Jasperson woman casts a weird mien. No doubt she's trouble."

"In fact, dear, this whole evening has been weird. It started with that partially dressed Chinese woman, Mae whatever her name is, asking too many questions. The French actress pretending that she was onstage and the lounge car was a burlesque house. That 'stiff upper lip' British officer and his stoic wife husbanding that stripper. And that Italian couple—I doubt that they are even married. Those female collegiates—irritating and out of place on this train. The only person whom I suspect is authentic is that mandarin—at least he was not pretentious and kept to himself."

"All true, husband." She taps his valise resting on the dresser. "This cash is just too dangerous for us to handle in this bandit country. We should have had a bank draft or something. Not so?"

"No, my dear. Our contact insisted on U.S. currency in gold notes. It's our only option."

"Then we've got to devise a plan to secrete these million dollars in case more trouble develops. As I'm sure it will. I feel it in my bones."

"You're probably correct, my dear. What do you suggest?"

The college girls retire to their quarters, inebriated and exhausted from their frenetic dancing. Too tired to change into night gowns, they plop into their beds with their clothes on.

Beams from the Shanghai Express's powerful light reflect off the steel trestles on the Grand Canal Bridge. The engineer blows the steam whistle a dozen times and rings the bell continuously. The train eases across the bridge.

七

Near Lincheng, Shantung Province.
0300 hours, 6 May 1923

As soon as the Shanghai Express's engine hits the sabotaged track, the right rail splays out widely. The train continues forward a few feet, then the engine and the coal car tip over to the right, slamming onto the ground, crushing the engineer and fireman. The boiler barrel bursts and superheated steam escapes. Soon, the engine explodes, scattering hot shrapnel that takes down a number of bandits. Fortunately, the new British breakaway turnbuckle on the Jenny coupler works as designed. Accordingly, the armored car, baggage car, and all the remaining cars remain upright on the tracks.

Throughout the train, the jolt slams the passengers about their compartments. None are hurt seriously, but all suffer bruises and lacerations. In the darkness of night, the bandits swarm down the embankments, yelling and firing their weapons helter-skelter.

The sudden jolt tosses Randolph and Maureen Van Halsted to the floor and into the forward bulkhead. "Maureen, you okay?" He kneels beside her. "Bandits are attacking."

She rubs her head and withdraws her bloody hand. "I hurt all over and this cut on my head is bleeding all over my new blouse." Randolph inspects Maureen's cut and sees that it is superficial, but a bleeder. He rips the sleeve off a white shirt and wraps it around her head.

Somewhat bewildered, she draws her Beretta and with false bravado says, "Let 'em come."

Randolph knows that time is pressing. "We've got to act now, Maureen. Else these scoundrels will steal our cache of money. Ideas?"

With Randolph's help, Maureen rises and sits in the lounge chair. In a few seconds, she shouts, "Indeed!" She jabs her right index finger at Randolph. "Tear these gold certificates into thirds and flush them in the toilet. Later, perhaps, we can recover the pieces. The Treasury Department will redeem these pieces and issue new certificates." With questioning eyes, she asks, "Their serial numbers are in the safe at your office? True? If we cannot recover the pieces, the Department will cancel these bills and issue new ones. Either way, we'll keep these certificates from those scoundrels."

Randolph remains silent as he evaluates her scheme. A couple of seconds later he exclaims, "Bravo! Terrific idea. Let's do it."

The derailment throws Jasperson headfirst into the forward wall and her Webley sails across the room. Lying on the floor, she rubs her head to ease the sting. Trying to recover, she hears the cacophony of multiple rifle reports and the harmonic chatter of machine-gun fire. *Damn. Bandits!* Her compartment window shatters as a bullet sails through and embeds in the opposite wall. She retrieves her gun, slides behind the lounge chair, and waits to assess the situation. *They'll not capture me alive. I'll take the bastards with me.*

The Gurkhas recover and return fire. Several dozen bandits drop. Unfortunately, the soldiers are seriously outnumbered and outgunned— the machine gun takes a terrible toll. Within a few minutes, their British officer and all the men are deadly quiet. With rich loot nearby, the bandits break discipline. The machine gunners and their crew swarm over the Gurkhas' bodies, grab their rifles and ammunition, steal their boots, and snatch their kukri knives and whirl them above their heads. Several don the soldiers' Kashmir hats and gambol in a mocking dance. Sergeant Tang Tse-che dons the officer's jacket and cap, and parades up and down beside the armored car, shouting inane commands to a phantom army.

A dozen bandits rush the baggage car, capture the two porters, and demand the keys to the safe and strong boxes. After looting the treasure troves, they ransack the car. They throw the suitcases and trunks to the ground and rip them open. They scatter their contents, wildly searching for items of value—those readily converted to cash or useful for favorable barter. One fellow wraps a *brassière* around his head and prances around. Others scatter the contents over a wide area and pick favored items.

The marauders fired dozens of rounds into the windows and directly into the compartments. Woozy, Nani Atticus wonders what the ruckus is about. He looks out the window and a bullet greets him. He slides to the bed and expires.

Now the bandits use the butts of their rifles to smash aisle windows and climb into the cars. Once inside, they open the cars' doors, run along the corridors, and begin rousting the passengers from their compartments.

Corporal Ts'zo Banh orders his squad to smash open the door to Todd and Laura Fleet's compartment. The pair are cowering on the floor behind the bed. Todd in pajamas, and Laura in a sheer peignoir, sans dainties. Ts'zo, with his Mauser semi-automatic pistol drawn, orders them with a hand motion to stand and come forward.

Todd, with a stumbling voice, says, "Go away. Leave us alone. We've nothing for you. We are medical missionaries." He shakes his fist at the corporal. "Get out."

The fellow does not understand English, but he does understand body motion and the tone of voice of an arrogant, Western imperialist. With his black eyes blazing, he jams the butt of his rifle across Todd's face. Todd slips to the floor and moans in intense pain as blood oozes from his mouth and nose.

Laura is quick to assess the scene and decides that to do nothing is her optimum strategy. *It's best to be kidnapped and survive. I'll be ransomed and can continue my life—probably without Todd.*

Unfortunately, she grossly overestimates the bandit's chivalry.

Ts'zo shouts an order to a private. The bandit grabs Laura's arms, twists them behind her, and ties them with stout twine. Ts'zo rips off her peignoir and throws her on the bed.

She screams and screams.

A clique of the blackguards force open the lounge car's rear door and spill into the bar. In a *mêlée*, they grab liquor bottles, knock off their necks, and drink recklessly.

Throughout the ambush, Sun tries to maintain control of his bandit gang, but is only marginally successful. His carefully constructed discipline culture is evaporating. He knows that ransom for the Occidental passengers has the greatest value, and hostages ensure safe conduct from pursuing soldiers—this time the pursuing soldiers probably will be revenge-seeking British Commonwealth troops. However, the lure of immediate treasure and nubile white women is too compelling for him to counter his men's fanatical frenzy.

Mandarin Fu Kuang-hsű clearly understands the developing scenario and knows exactly what to do. He unlocks his door and pushes his two nude concubines into the hall. They are captured immediately and are viciously banged about as the bandits fight to possess them. Unfamiliar with this harsh treatment, they look back at Fu and their eyes plead for rescue. He ignores them. Fu shouts an order to the mob brawling over the women.

Lieutenant Yang Hasi-peng hears Fu's order and fights his way through the rumpus. Immediately, he recognizes Fu as a nabob, an important mandarin—it is his imperious command of the language, and cavalier attitude in sacrificing his concubines.

Fu addresses Yang. "I must assume that this raid is the work of the bandit Sun Mei-yao of Shantung Province. Not so?"

"Yes, Mandarin. It is Sun." Now it is evident clearly to Yang that this fellow is a powerful man with many connections and should not be harassed or harmed.

"Tell Sun that Fu Kuang-hsű, of Peiping, would wish to speak with him. I will wait in my compartment. Meanwhile, command your ruffians to stay away."

"Yes, Mandarin. I will see to it."

At the sound of the first shot, Mae Ling-weh grabs her diary, turns over the dresser, and slides to the floor behind it. The firing continues unabated and several bullets smash into her window and embed in the furniture. Several minutes later, her door bursts open and Captain Chao Tan-keng rushes in with his Mauser at the ready. In the dark, he spots Mae but cannot discern her features. "Come to me, woman," he demands.

Mae, in her gossamer thin negligee, rises and responds, "Yes, sir." She saunters to him. Her Chanel No. 5 perfume engulfs Chao. She moves the Mauser to his side, and wraps her arms around him. "Captain Chao, I did not expect that it would be you to enter my compartment." She wiggles against him. "You are most welcome." She kisses him full on the mouth with intense passion.

Chao, no fool, recognizes Mae and shoves her away. "Enough, wanton! Sun is waiting for your report."

Karina exclaims, "They're just outside our compartment."

Over the din, Ashley-Cooper speaks loudly. "Well, ol' girl, looks as if we'll use those self-defense weapons sooner than expected." Ashley-Cooper drops open the cylinder on his Webley. All cartridges are in place. He grasps his sword cane in his left hand. "Karina, you understand that I cannot be captured. I hold many of the Crown's secrets. We'll fight our way out of this mess. With me?"

Tears begin to flood Karina's cheeks as she realizes the enormity of their dire situation. "Of course, ol' man. For King and Country." She grasps tightly her Webley. "I'm ready."

"I'll pop the door open. We'll hit the aisle on our knees. You take the right side. I'm left. Now, a deep breath, love." He kisses her on the cheek. "On my count. Here we go. One, two, three." The pair spill into the aisle, which is crowded with bandits. Within a few seconds, twelve of the fellows lie dead and block the way. Karina reloads and continues firing, using the bodies as a shield. Out of ammunition, Ashley-Cooper draws the rapier from his sword cane and runs it through the heart of the nearest bandit. The fellow behind the falling bandit fires his pistol at Ashley-Cooper, hitting him high in his torso. The wounded major kneels down and keels over—his life force ebbing.

In the *mêlée*, Karina, unaware of Quentin's fate, continues firing. A bullet slams into her chest. She collapses and blood pumps slowly from her wound.

Corporal Ts'zo Banh sees her lying on the floor and bleeding. He concludes that she will soon die and they do not need old, wrinkled women. He and his men ransack Ashley-Cooper's compartment. The particular treasure is Major Ashley-Cooper's mess dress uniform.

Jasperson hears the ruckus in the hallway, a female scream, and what she assumes is return fire from different caliber guns. The firing from the compartment side of the train ceases. What firing there is, is coming from the aisle side of the coaches. There is intense pounding on her door and she sees the hinges beginning to give. With no other option, she peeks out the shattered compartment window. No bandits are in sight, and directly below is a mound that is a couple of feet high. With the butt of her Webley, she smashes the window and climbs out. Several remaining shards slice her, others break off into her body. Her door flies open and several bandits rush in. Instead of running to hide, she turns toward the broken window and sees the bandits sacking her room. *Damn! I'm not going to let those bastards destroy my property.* She sights her Webley and squeezes six rounds. Six bandits drop. She turns and runs zigzag up the embankment and return fire follows, zinging around her head and kicking dirt particles up into the air. Rounding the top of the rise, she falls to the ground and hides behind tall bushes. She looks toward the train below and sees that no one is following her. She catches her breath and fumes, *Damn fool! MI6 agent Jasperson, that was stupid. Your high dudgeon overcame your better judgment.* She picks pieces of glass out of her arms, knees, and legs. *So, fire me, Controller James.* She grabs six cartridges from her pocket and reloads. *For now, I'll remain here and reconnoiter the unfolding scene below.*

Sun knocks furtively on Fu's door and says softly, "Mandarin Fu Kuang-hsǔ, I am the bandit Sun Mei-yao responding to your request for a conversation." He recognizes that he is in a difficult situation. He dare not harm or offend Fu—he is too powerful and has influence in all quarters of government.

There is a long pause; finally, through the door Sun hears, "If you are he, you may enter." Sun opens the door gently and steps softly into Fu's compartment. "Greetings, Mandarin Fu. I am pleased to confer with you."

Fu evaluates Sun in person. For several years, Fu has been following this bandit's career as reported in newspapers, and he is impressed. "You may sit, bandit."

With as much deference as he can muster, Sun responds, "Mandarin Fu, I have the greatest respect for you." He squirms in his seat. "Unfortunately, to uphold my reputation I must ask for a token ransom. I'm sure you understand."

"Money, is it?"

"If you would be so kind."

"How many dollars would suffice?"

"Mandarin Fu, not Chinese funny money, please." Phrasing his request as carefully as he can, Sun asks, "May we consider British pounds sterling?"

"Not satisfactory."

"Then, gold. A few ounces."

"Not satisfactory," Fu snaps. "Bandit Sun, I would suggest something more valuable. On my release and safe return to Peiping, I will send you twelve kilos of pure opium paste and six beautiful young women from my own compound—well trained in the erotic arts."

Shocked at such a generous offer, Sun responds, "I am truly grateful, Mandarin." Sun smiles inwardly. His stars doubly shine on him today. "Your ransom is satisfactory."

"Then we have an agreement." Fu stands and addresses Sun in his most imperious voice. "However, there is a proviso, Sun Mei-yao. Henceforth, you are part of my organization and will do my bidding." Fu, with almost ceremonial aplomb, crosses his arms and slides them into the open sleeves of his dress. "This contract extends indefinitely." He stares at Sun with his intense black eyes. "Should you default in any manner, you, and all you hold dear, will beg me for a quicker death." He pauses for impact. "Are my terms worthy?"

Shaken to his core at Fu's outrageous demand, Sun realizes that he has no options. To defy Fu would earn a three-day crucifixion—after many other tortures. Resigned, he responds, "Mandarin Fu, your contract terms are indeed satisfactory. I am humbled to be in your service."

Xenia De Luca stands on the tracks with the *attaché* case tucked tightly under her left arm, and watches the Shanghai Express cross the Grand Canal Bridge. She decides that after the train is long out of sight, she'll make her way to Lincheng and catch a southbound train to Shanghai. *Then I am to the Americas on the first outbound tramp steamer.* Suddenly, the opening racket of the ambush startles her. A few stray bullets ping off the girders. Instantly, she recognizes what is happening and sprints down the railroad tracks away from the bridge. Spotting a large group of bulrushes, she dives inside for cover. Unfortunately, the cobra did not want company. Her screams are not heard.

Resigned, Randolph tells Maureen, "We've no option. Throw your pistol on the bed. We must give up. My lawyer will pay whatever ransom they demand." He tosses his diamond-studded watch and a ruby ring in the commode. There is pounding on their door. "Quick wife, toss as much of your jewelry as possible in the toilet and flush it." She complies as the pounding on the door increases.

She quickly places her two family heirlooms—a diamond wedding ring and an emerald broach—in her hair bun and wraps it with a cotton scarf.

"Be careful. Do not let an unguarded comment reveal our true wealth." He raises his hands in the universal gesture of "I surrender." She follows his lead.

Sun rises from Mae's bed and puts on his uniform. With authority, he demands, "Give me your diary and review your notations." He realizes that with his men on a rampage, he has little chance to recover any significant jewelry or cash. Those that are fortunate enough to secure treasures will desert and scatter throughout the provinces. Ransom seems to be the only profitable option. "Tell me which passengers have the most assets to pay my demands."

Dutifully, Mae recites her observations regarding the passengers' wealth, including the identities of those who wore expensive jewelry.

"As usual, you've done well. You'll get your percentage when all is collected and I've sold what jewelry I recover."

Neither is aware of the true nature of the chaos his men have caused or of the number of passengers who are dead or seriously wounded.

Mae has made a rough calculation of the total value of this raid. "Sun, you will reap a handsome profit from this morning's business. I deserve a much higher percentage than usual."

Sun has used Mae several times to fine measure as his intelligence agent. But he will not honor her demand. "No. We made a deal and we will stay with it."

Mae does not acquiesce readily. "Sun, I have done loyal work often enough for you to know that I am thoroughly reliable. Because your rogue bandits almost killed me with their reckless rifle fire, this assignment was especially hazardous. I demand more."

He looks at her with unbelieving eyes. Women do not demand from him. "No!" He turns to leave her compartment. "Your next assignment will be ready shortly."

"Bandit, you do not hear me. I want more." Her eyes flash with anger. "Else I will notify the Western authorities."

Sun's ire rises. He does not suffer fools gladly. He draws his saber and slashes her neck. Her headless body convulses and collapses to the ground. He holsters his saber and whispers, "Not today, Mistress Mae. My new Peiping agent will take control of your Bamboo restaurant and the remainder of your assets."

The collegiate girls are giddy with excitement. Melinda offers, "Just imagine the thrill of being captured by real-live Chinese bandits—just like in the movies. How rousing it will be to tell all our classmates next semester."

Bertie adds, "My dad could make a thrilling movie about us." She twirls around. "We could play ourselves. We'll get Mary Pickford to play that Jasperson woman. Anna May Wong to be that Eurasian woman, Mae Ling-wei or whatever her name is. And Lon Chaney as the bandit leader. Oh! It will be a great film."

Even as the bandits pound on their door, the coeds laugh, dance about, and hug each other. Thea is dour and does not partake in the coed nonsense. Her father is in the Foreign Service and was posted to China when she was in her early teens. She has an inkling of what awaits them as bandit prisoners. She shouts over the ruckus, "Stop it, you fools. We are in terrible danger. Calm yourselves. Face these fellows forthrightly as American citizens under the protection of the Stars and Stripes."

In unison, the coeds give Thea a boisterous raspberry.

The bandits break down the door. They are awe-struck and exceptionally quiet at the Occidental treasures they have found. Sergeant Hsu Su-en immediately takes command and orders the men to stand at attention. He knows that Sun would want these women unharmed so that he can command high ransoms, or sell them to warlords for exorbitant prices. Hsu assumes, *probably all virgins*. Naturally, he would get a handsome bonus for finding them and bringing them to Sun in pristine condition.

Mindy exclaims with ineffable awe, "Are we really captured by bandits and having the thrill of a lifetime?"

"Shut up, *estúpido*," shouts Thea. "Indeed you are, and that 'thrill' will soon turn into unmitigated horror."

One private, an especially aggressive fellow, breaks ranks, rushes to buxom Thea, and begins to rip off her blouse. She backs a step, and with all her might kicks the fellow in his groin. He screams in excruciating pain and crumples to floor with both his hands grasping his wound.

Thea shouts at him, "You addlebrained bastard. Best to leave Occidental woman alone—especially Tejana women. We're not the compliant ninnies your women are." In her most distinctive West Texas drawl, tinged with a Spanish accent, she continues, "We don't 'cotton' to ungentlemanly conduct. *¿Comprende? Bastardo!*"

Sergeant Hsu does not understand her words, but her action speaks volumes. He cannot tolerate such dissension from prisoners. It is a black mark on his leadership. He whips his pistol onto the side of Thea's face. Without a sound, she crumples to the floor and a large gash begins to bleed profusely.

The girls scream as the reality of their capture is so graphically demonstrated. The sergeant prevents them from tending to Thea. Instead, at gun point, his men hustle the coeds out of the compartment. Sergeant Hsu glances at Thea and concludes that she is not worth the trouble of carrying. She is skinny, ugly, and dying.

Near Lincheng, Shantung Province.
0600 hours, 6 May 1923

Chaos reigns around the wrecked Shanghai Express. Bandits, in a *mêlée* of frantic enthusiasm, randomly fire their rifles into the air to celebrate of their successful raid: revenge on Western imperialists, rich loot, rapine, and the capture of wealthy Occidentals. Some bandits continue to plunder, taking with them anything that seems valuable. Now, however, some three hours later, little booty remains.

The once elegant British train lies in ruins; the engine is destroyed and the baggage car is ransacked. Bandits have captured attendants, murdered several first-class passengers, kidnapped others, and raped a married woman. They have stripped the living compartments of anything of potential worth, stolen silver from the dining car, and smashed the dinnerware and the crystal. They've consumed or stolen expensive wine and liquor, and spilled it on expensive carpets.

Sun rages in frustration at the debacle of his once keenly disciplined bandit gang, now in disarray. He and his officers try to organize his men into some semblance of an orderly military formation, but only several dozen privates and all his noncommissioned officers comply.

His officers shout, "Fall in! Fall in!" but without much success.

Sun shouts at the top of his voice, "Sons of donkeys, fall in!"

Surprisingly, most of his troops ignore his commands—some are drunk, many are exhilarated to inanity, and others continue their celebration and flash expensive jewelry. As he sees his command authority quickly eroding, Sun explodes in anger. He draws his Mauser pistol, fires several rounds into the air, and hollers, "Within two minutes, I'll shoot any man who is not in formation."

The men know that Sun's threats are always deadly serious—the celebration grinds to a halt. Exhausted, the men begin to obey.

Captain Chao Tan-keng, Sun's executive officer, commands, "Attention!"

The men align themselves as best they can and develop a semblance of a military formation. Sun reviews what is left of his once large and well-ordered force, now reduced to a dwarfed, ragtag gang of looters. Crestfallen, he demands from Captain Chao Tan-keng, "Where are my men, my army of notorious bandits?"

Captain Chao salutes and, with trepidation, answers, "Many are dead. Several are seriously wounded and cannot make muster." He points in several directions to bandits scurrying away. "Many others, heady with loot, are deserting."

Sun, not to be challenged, proclaims, "When we find a deserter, I will crucify him."

Captain Chao continues, "The shrapnel from the exploding engine killed seven or eight. The Gurkhas' counter-fire accounted for almost thirty of our men, and wounded many more." Knowing that Sun is prone to killing the messenger of bad news, he steels the last of his dram of courage and continues, "Surprisingly, Commander Sun, some of the passengers were well-armed, and fought bravely. They killed almost twenty and wounded others—some seriously." He takes a deep breath. "Lastly, our men fought among themselves over the concubines and nine or ten were killed."

Sun, stunned that months of training and strict discipline have failed, exclaims, "Stupid peasants! If we find any of the men who killed over these whores, they will die painfully."

One drunken bandit approaches the line whilst rubbing, of all things, toothpaste on his face. Sun shoots him in both knees. "Idiot!"

The sun is several degrees above the horizon and bright light floods the area. Sun knows that he must complete his tasks at the wreck quickly, and then depart for his hideout. He does not know when the alarm will sound, but knows it will not be long before the local militia is organized and begins its pursuit. *The condition of my men and those Occidental prisoners will cause trouble and slow us to a crawl.* He orders Sergeant Tang to force the prisoners into a line on the embankment.

Tang soon has the captives standing shoulder to shoulder, including Randolph and Maureen Van Halsted, Mindy, Bertie, Bonny, and Melinda. Next to Melinda are the two baggage-car porters.

Sun is puzzled at the paucity of the prisoners. According to Mae's diary, there should be about three times as many. "Where are all the Occidentals? There ought to be many more." He carefully scrutinizes the prisoners in the line, comparing them to those listed in Mae's diary. Not satisfied, he demands, "For instance, where is the British major and his wife…and…that older British woman? I see the Italian and his woman are missing. There should be a Russian, a French movie actress, some American adventuress, and an American missionary and his wife. Where are these people? What has happened to them? I see only four American college students. Where is the fifth? And where is the porter? I do not understand. I staged this raid to capture a host of Occidentals for a rich ransom, and I'm left with this motley crew."

He stomps away to collect his thoughts. He turns and shouts, "Captain Chao, order the men to stand easy." *At least I know from Mae's diary that the older American couple are rich and, I suspect, so are the families of those college girls. Perhaps I can make something of this fiasco after all.*

A villainous-looking bandit, sodden from the stolen liquor, prances in front of the prisoners. He is wearing a string of pearls and two wristwatches. Because Sun needs all the men he can get, he forgoes serious punishment. He shouts, "Sergeant Tang, get that man in formation, strip him of that loot, and slap him with all your might."

Inwardly, he is worried. Without his army, his position is precarious. *Rivals will attack me and Mandarin Fu expects me to have a fully functioning and disciplined army that can serve him.* He returns to the formation and orders all his noncommissioned officers to break rank and to find and return deserters. To any deserters who obey his command, he offers immunity and half of the booty they have recovered. "Those who disobey I will consider outcasts and when captured they will suffer on the cross."

He grabs Captain Chao by the arm. "Let us inspect the wounded. You go inside the train. I will do the grounds. Get those who are ambulatory into the formation—our medical people will treat them. Administer the *coup de grâce* for the seriously wounded—we have no time or facilities for them."

Over the next few minutes, the prisoners, and those bandits in formation, hear many of the Mauser's familiar pops.

Overwhelmed with this ongoing scenario, Sun has deferred action regarding Mandarin Fu. He orders Lieutenant Yang Hasi-peng to ride into Lincheng and commandeer an automobile to drive Mandarin Fu Kuang-hsü to Peiping.

Sun then hustles to Fu's compartment. "My sincere apologies, Mandarin Fu." Sun speaks with servile deference to the nabob. "I have been occupied with pressing matters trying to organize the chaos in the aftermath of my raid. I've sent for an automobile to transport you to Peiping."

Fu responds, "It is none too quickly, bandit Sun. You have left me in this dreadful place. Already the stink of the dead offends my nostrils. Flies, with all manner of diseases, land on my face and hands." He rises from the chair, exits the coach, and ambles toward the prisoners.

Sun follows, chagrined at his lapse of attention toward the nabob, and offers, "Would you care to enjoy the company of one of those young Occidental women while en route to Peiping? Perhaps two?"

Fu takes the measure of the four collegiates standing in the line. They are obviously distraught—several are sobbing, their clothes are in disarray from rough handling, and their overall mien does not present a pleasant image. "No. I have no taste for Occidental women. They are disobedient, smell of Western imperialism, ugly, and not sensuous while in congress."

Sun responds patronizingly, "You speak wisely, Mandarin."

The prisoners wonder why the other Occidentals are not in line with them. "Randolph, do you have any idea where the rest of our friends are?" Maureen whispers.

"Not a clue, Maureen. And it would be best to remain quiet. If any speak English, I'm not aware of it. Nonetheless, speak softly and politely when required. So far, they have done very well with body language and their guns."

To Maureen Van Halsted's horror, she spots a bandit wearing Bridget von Cairo's blue georgette hat. She wonders why Bridget is not in the line.

Meanwhile, Captain Chao had been talking with the men about the missing Occidentals. He now approaches Sun. "Sir, if I may, I have information about the absent Westerners. I cannot say with absolute confidence that it is correct, but it is what the men tell me."

The bandit leader glances at the sky and notices that the sun is much higher. He stamps his right foot impatiently and demands, "Speak!"

Knowing of Sun's fierce demand for accuracy, he speaks distinctly. "Our men killed the British major and his wife in self-defense. These two militarists were responsible for nineteen or twenty of our losses."

Fu mumbles, "I shall light a joss stick at our shrine and curse their British ancestors. Continue."

"It appears that the Italian man was killed by a stray bullet. His woman is missing, and none of the Occidentals know of her whereabouts. Shall I continue?"

"Hurry. We must move out of this cursed place. The militia will be after us shortly."

"Yes, sir. Sergeant Hsu Su-en killed the missing college girl, because she assaulted one of his private soldiers and threatened others. She was a madwoman. He is justified." He shuffles his feet to gather composure and phrase his next words most carefully. "Corporal Ts'zo Banh and his squad entered the compartment of the missionary, Fleet, and his wife. Unfortunately, his wife was dressed most provocatively. As a result, he and his men had their way with her. She went into a stupor with dead eyes. Her husband tried to interfere and Corporal Ts'zo smashed his head with the butt of his rifle. He left them there because she would no longer have value, and the man was dead."

Almost unbelieving this last story because of his strict instructions to forgo rape of the Occidental women, Sun demands, "Bring Corporal Ts'zo and his squad here."

The squad is soon standing at attention in front of Sun. For a long while he says nothing as he looks deeply at each man. Finally, he says, "About face. Kneel down and bow your heads." He draws his Mauser and executes the corporal and moves to the next man with his pistol at the ready.

Captain Chao taps Sun's right elbow slightly, "Sir, forgive me for interfering. We need these men. Our losses were heavy today."

Sun looks at Chao with threatening eyes. Several seconds later, he relaxes. "Indeed, you are correct, Captain. When we return to camp, have these men flogged."

"Shall I complete my report?"

"Yes. Get on with it."

"The mature British woman escaped through her window, killed five of our men, and seriously wounded another." He looks at his notes to ensure that his next report will be correct. "The remaining Occidentals are missing without a trace, and no one knows about them. They are as follows: the French actress, the Russian, the American woman who was traveling alone. I should add that the porter, Rahman, also cannot be found."

Sun cocks his head in disbelief. "How can all these people disappear without a trace? What great mystery has engulfed this cursed train—the Shanghai Express? People do not just vanish. Is it possessed of demons?"

他處.

From her hiding place, Jasperson keeps watch on the activities around the wrecked Shanghai Express. Eventually, she sees the bandits and hostages leave. She waits until late afternoon, deciding then that it is safe to inspect the train. The onlookers have left and the few militiamen guarding the train are in the baggage car, waste-picking what scrap remains. She crawls out of her hiding place and cautiously approaches the train wreck.

With her Webley at the ready, Jasperson walks to the back of the train and is shocked at the carnage—several dozen bandit bodies are strewn haphazardly around the area. Already, the flies have arrived, she notes. She climbs the rear platform and enters the train through the lounge car. She gasps at the butchery of the corpses that block the aisle; the stink of decaying bodies nearly overwhelms her. A legion of flies buzz her.

Keeping her handkerchief over her mouth and nose, she moves adroitly down the littered corridors and peeks into her compartment. The disarray is appalling. *What the hell. Those porcine animals.* She enters what's left of her compartment. Pale sunlight casts enough light through the smashed window for her to see. She rips off the bathroom mirror, reaches her hand into a secret compartment, and retrieves her passports, currency in British pounds sterling, and the nearly worthless Chinese dollars—as well as a small leather pouch of Edward V gold sovereigns. She finds only one slightly soiled dress in the pile on the floor and a pair of walking shoes. She changes and, with adhesive tape, secures her documents and the currency to her inner thighs. Then she drops the pouch into a side pocket of her dress and secures it with a safety pin.

Jasperson passes the collegiates' room and, through the open door, hears a faint moan. She enters and spots Thea sprawled in the lounge chair. Streams of dried blood have caked on her face, and spittle is oozing from her lips as she labors to breathe through her mouth. Thea tries to speak, but cannot. Instead, she blinks her eyes several times, which speaks of her intense pain.

"My God! Thea!" Jasperson exclaims. "Be calm. We're safe. The bandits have left. Let me see to your wounds." She inspects Thea's trauma—her jaw is broken, the deep gash needs cleaning and sutures, her nose is askew and probably also broken. Alarmed, Jasperson kisses Thea gently on her forehead. "Hang tough, Texan. I'm going to my compartment. I'll be back."

Jasperson enters her compartment, sticks her hand under the bed and, much to her surprise, finds her first-aid kit intact. She climbs over bodies strewn along the corridor and returns to Thea's compartment. "Lie back, young woman. I'll tend to you as best I can." She digs in her first-aid kit and takes out her emergency morphine bottle and a syringe. "Keep the faith."

With pleading eyes, Thea struggles to lift her hand to touch Jasperson's face. Within seconds after the injection, her hand falls aimlessly. Thea closes her eyes, and drifts off into a deep sleep.

Jasperson shakes her head in disbelief. *What madness is this?* She applies the experimental drug sulfonamide to Thea's wounds, and applies dressings. She is flummoxed, *Why was Thea not kidnapped? Instead she is severely wounded.* A puzzlement. Speaking aloud, she says in a soft voice, "Sleep peacefully, dear flapper. You are in my charge."

Back in the hall, she hears a weak female voice call out. She advances almost to the opposite end of the car and sees the wounded Karina Ashley-Cooper sitting on the floor next to the prone Major Ashley-Cooper. Jasperson climbs over the stack of bandit bodies to reach Karina. She sees a small stream of blood pumping out of Karina's blouse. Her face is ashen.

With effort Karina whispers, "I'm cold." The pumping blood from her chest wound oozes heavily.

At the sight of this carnage, the hard-boiled Jasperson wipes tears from her cheeks. She assesses Karina's wound and her affect. She looks directly into Karina's eyes, and slowly shakes her head from side to side.

Karina forces a faint smile of understanding. A faint sparkle appears in her eyes, and she purposely lies back on the body of her husband.

Jasperson kneels and gently closes Karina's eyes. Her hard-boiled mien crumbles at the appalling scene. Mighty sobs of bitter grief rise from her soul. She struggles to keep her composure—and fails. Within a few seconds, she recovers and surveys the scene. She notes the pistol in Karina's hand, the rapier in a bandit's heart, the great number of brass cases strewn about the area. Her heart swells with pride, and she gives a snappy salute. She says, almost as a prayer, "Keener the heart, the greater the courage." She bows her head. *Quentin and Karina Ashley-Cooper, you have served King and Country with exceptional valor in defense of Empire. I shall include an account of your courage in my report and recommend the King's honors for both of you brave Britons.*

On a hunch that there might be more wounded passengers, Jasperson enters the forward car. All manner of clothes, furniture, and accessories are strewn about. About midway, she passes the Fleets' compartment. The door hangs at an angle. She looks inside and sees the nude Laura sitting on the bed, staring into space with dead eyes. The mattress under her is soaked in blood. Nearby, Todd lies motionless on the floor. She checks, and sees that his skull is smashed and he has no pulse. *Damn!* Laura's trauma is readily apparent. Jasperson retrieves a glass of water and encourages her to drink.

Some life returns to Laura's eyes and she blinks in acknowledgment. Several seconds later, she speaks in a faint voice. "I'm cold. Very cold."

Gravely concerned by Laura's loss of blood, Jasperson responds, "Laura, dear, I'm going to tend to you. Understand?" As carefully as she can, she helps Laura to lie on the bed and covers her with a light blanket.

Laura mumbles almost unintelligibly, "Pain. Awful."

Jasperson says, almost in a whisper, "Soon it will fade." She injects morphine into Laura's right arm and says softly, "This opiate will ease your pain."

It acts so quickly that Laura does not hear her.

As carefully as she can, Jasperson applies the sulfonamide powder to Laura's privates. She applies gauze infused with a sulfa drug to Laura's bruised and bloody face, and dabs iodine and the sulfa to the many open wounds on Laura's body. Jasperson whispers to the unconscious victim, "I'm going for help and will be back as soon as I can."

Jasperson exits, and sees a squad of Nationalist militia troops marching quick-time toward the train. They quickly establish a cordon around the train, keeping looters and sightseers away.

An Occidental civilian approaches Jasperson and in a clipped Australian accent asks, "You are a surviving passenger?"

"Yes. I have two seriously wounded women on board and they need immediate medical treatment." Surprised to see an English speaker in this remote province, she asks, "Who are you?"

"I am the stationmaster at Lincheng." He looks at the chaos surrounding the Shanghai Express. "I am Charles Farmer, from Goolwa, South Australia—'down under' to you 'pommies.'" He speaks to a young man standing beside him. The fellow runs toward the town. "My man, Yeh, will return shortly with an ambulance and our doctor—a Chinese man of fine reputation—Doctor Ch'in Pang-hsien. He is skilled in Western medicine and Oriental remedies."

Annoyed, Jasperson spouts, "I don't give a damn what technique he uses. He's got to get these women stable and ready for transport to Shanghai. They will need blood. When is the next southbound train due?"

"The local should be here in a couple of hours—never can tell, exactly. Don't recommend it—it's far too slow." He withdraws his railroad pocket watch. "The southbound Shanghai Express is due at 2006 hours. However, it does not stop at Lincheng." He looks westward and points to a weed-covered area about one hundred yards away. "With the main track splayed and blocked with the wreckage of the Shanghai Express, we'll switch rail traffic to that abandoned track over there. It's okay. We checked it a few days ago. Of course, all traffic will crawl its way to the bridge."

Frustrated to a nearly uncontrolled anger, Jasperson demands, "I do not give a good bloody damn what the schedule is, or what track it's on. Stop that southbound Express" She jabs her index finder at him. "Have a compartment ready with two hospital beds, and a doctor. Understand, Aussie?"

"Indeed, I do, madam. I will get on the telegraph straight away. By the by, whom do I charge for these expenses?"

Unable to believe Farmer's pecuniary request at this critical time, she snaps, "Send the bill to me, Margaret Jasperson, at the American Express Office, Peiping. I take personal responsibility. Also, there are five bodies that need service, a British Officer and his wife, a doctor missionary, an Italian industrialists, and a Chinese woman. Also, bury the gurkhas soldiers in the local cemetery. I'll make arrangements with British officials for their burial with proper military honors. I don't give a damn what you do with the bodies of those bandits."

"I will take care of it." He surveys the wreckage of the northbound Shanghai Express. "My superiors will be most displeased, mate."

地陪

Railroad Station, Lincheng, Shantung Province.
2014 hours, 6 May 1923

Amid a cacophony of screeching, clanging, and bell ringing, the southbound Shanghai Express screeches to a stop. The conductor swings out from one of the executive coaches and demands of stationmaster Farmer, "Are the patients ready? We are late, and we have lots of time to make up due to this unauthorized stop on our schedule."

Jasperson, with her Webley tucked into her belt, responds, "Patience, Conductor. They are coming out of the waiting room."

Chinese porters carry the litters with Laura and Thea to the train. Blood transfusions have returned color to the patients' cheeks. Both are still groggy from the second dose of morphine—this one administered by Doctor Ch'in. He follows his patients to the train.

Jasperson, Doctor Ch'in, Farmer, and the Chinese porters, as gently as possible, hustle the patients into beds in a specially prepared compartment.

Towards the baggage car, several men push a large baggage wagon loaded with five simple pine coffins—two are covered with the Union Jack, one with the Stars and Stripes, one with a charcoal-scrawled fasces, and the other with the ideographs for "Chinese."

As soon as Farmer and the Chinese porters depart, the conductor blows his whistle in several long bursts and vigorously waves the red flag over his head. He swings aboard. Amid a cloud of steam and vigorous bell ringing, the Shanghai Express gains purchase and inches forward.

地陪

Margaret Jasperson knows that her aggressive conduct during the raid has compromised her career as a MI6 agent. She must avoid foreign intelligence services and the press at all costs. She knows it would be best to fade into obscurity before the authorities and the reporters start asking pointed questions that she knows she cannot answer.

The southbound Shanghai Express begins to increase its forward motion for the nonstop high-speed run to Shanghai. She knows that her charges are in the capable hands of Doctor Ch'in. Stationmaster Farmer has alerted railroad management in Shanghai, and ambulances and medical personnel will be waiting to accompany the patients to Mercy Catholic Hospital.

There is nothing more she can do and to tarry would be dangerous. Without a word, she exits the compartment, swings off the train at a run, and dashes for the brush at the base of the rise.

प

En route to the Patu-ku Mountains, Shantung Province.
1400 hours, 6–7 May 1923

Sun fumes at the slow pace in which the caravan is moving toward his hideaway—a long-abandoned Buddhist monastery deep in the remote Patu-ku Mountains. At spots, the trail is narrow and rough, and the caravan moves even more slowly. Sun knows that speed is essential because he must outpace his pursuers. Once safely inside his compound, he will be secure. Its only entrance is through a steep-faced, twisted, narrow cut in the granite mountain. His redoubt is almost impenetrable.

He fights his inner compulsion to kick his horse into a gallop and race far ahead. He's carrying in his saddlebags what loot he could garner: a reasonable jewelry collection including three strings of pearls, an emerald broach, and a collection of diamonds, sapphire rings, and several expensive watches. Instead of galloping, he turns around and rides down the length of the plodding column. Leading it are the mounted, bedraggled remnants of his once-feared bandit gang. Following them are several horse-drawn wagons. One carries the hostages; three are loaded with booty: clothing, shoes, dinnerware, cooking utensils, toiletries—anything of potential value, even mattresses; and the last two hold the implements of war, including his German machine gun. Sun has to make a decision. Several minutes ago, his rear guard scouts reported that the militia, reinforced with a platoon of Nationalist soldiers, had left Lincheng and started pursuit.

Captain Chao Tan-keng rides close. "Sir, we must take a break. The horses and men are exhausted."

"Not possible. We continue."

"Bandit Sun, if we do not break soon, what semblance of order our caravan still has will disappear into anarchy."

"No! The militia is following." *If I had my regular bandit gang, then we would make a stand in a defensive position and wipe out the pursuers.*

"Commander, water is essential for our animals and men. All need sustenance, now."

"No. We continue."

"If we do not stop now and refresh, all we fought for will be lost. The men will mutiny, kill the prisoners and us, share the spoils, and disappear. Many of our horses will drop. Hear me! Perchance we survive, Mandarin Fu will find us no matter where we would hide."

Reflecting on the wisdom of his executive officer, Sun complies in a resigned voice. "Very well. Make it a one-hour break. Afterwards, we have to move faster. I want to cross that roaring stream before dark."

He dismounts, leans against a tree, snacks on biscuits and hardtack, and takes a deep drink from his canteen. With all the turmoil, death, and paucity of expensive loot and prisoners, he wonders, *What demons have cursed this expedition? I, a top graduate of the Whampoa Military Academy, planned this attack with geometrical precision. Why have unknown demons thwarted me to shameful failure?*

He rises and walks about the campsite. His brain whirls with negative thoughts. Foremost is concern for the near future, when the professional soldiers will pursue him and try to rescue the hostages. *Nationalist troops from Shanghai and Nanching will soon follow. Within a few days, British colonial troops will be on the scene, and with Nepalese Gurkhas seeking blood revenge. Perhaps there will be American Marines from their security duties in the International Settlement in Shanghai.* His anxiety rises and beads of perspiration appear on his forehead. *My predicament is critical. What are my options?* He reckons that if they do not pick up the pace, it will take them another day or two to reach the security of his compound.

池阝号

Later in the day, the prisoners' wagon hits a large rock. The wheel shatters into wooden splinters, and the axel snaps. The prisoners are tossed to the ground. None are hurt seriously, but Maureen Van Halsted and coeds Mindy and Bonny sustain large bruises. Randolph helps Maureen and the collegiates recover. The Chinese porters shake away any attempt to help.

Sun dashes to the accident, dismounts, surveys the mishap, and cries, "Demon, what tribute do you demand? How may I satisfy your vengeance?" He orders the drovers, "Fix the wagon promptly. We must continue apace. Understand?"

With downcast eyes, the senior drover responds, "Bandit Sun, we are helpless. We cannot repair this wagon. We have no replacement wheel or axle. Please recall, that you ordered us to leave behind all extra equipment."

Confounded by his own words, his anger explodes and he shouts, "Demon, curse your ancestors!" He draws his pistol, intent on shooting the two drovers. In an instant, he understands the folly of that action and holsters his weapon. He says, "Carry on," and then gallops toward Captain Chao who is leading the caravan. "Disaster in our caravan. The wagon with the Westerners is broken and cannot be repaired."

Chao signals for the caravan to halt. "Exceptionally dire news, sir. Your plan?"

"I ask you, Executive Officer, for your recommendation."

Chao considers the options. "At the moment, I do not have a viable plan." He pauses for a few seconds to organize his thoughts. With vigor he proposes, "Let us split our force. I realize that such an option is against all sound military tactics. In these adverse circumstances, we might have a better chance of success."

Intrigued by such an unorthodox recommendation, Sun demands, "Continue."

"You take the body of our forces, move quickly, and prepare our sanctuary for the forthcoming siege. With the best squad we have, I will stay with the prisoners, and usher them along on foot. Should the pursuing soldiers close on us, they will not fire for fear of harming the Occidentals.

I can stall engagement until dark. Then, my squad and I will abandon the prisoners and meet you at our hideaway."

Sun walks about evaluating Chao's proposal. "I do not like the idea of abandoning our prisoners. They are our safety insurance and perhaps they might have serious worth for ransom. Nonetheless, I understand our liability with them walking." He continues his pacing. *That demon perplexes me. He must be a scholar, a patron of Robert Burns, to bedevil me so. 'The best laid schemes of mice and men.' is his hymn.*

Sun faces Captain Chao and says, "Very well. Reluctantly, I accept your scheme. However, I will keep one of the college girls. She will ride in one of the equipment wagons." Not caring who is selected, he orders Sergeant Tang Tse-che, "Choose one of the Occidental girls and force her into one of the equipment wagons. You will be her guard. Stay with her at all times. You know what will happen if she escapes."

"Yes, sir. I will comply."

Tang does not know why Sun wants one of these women, but suspects she is for his pleasure. Therefore, he chooses Bonny—the most attractive in his eyes. Without ado, he grabs her arm and pulls her upright.

"Stop it! What are you doing? Go away," shouts Bonny. She reaches for Mindy's arms and cries, "Help! This animal is hurting me."

The guard's strength overwhelms her and, with the point of his Mauser at the center of her back, he forces her to start walking to the front of the caravan. Her fear swells at the unknown, and she begins to sob uncontrollably as she moves at a stumbling pace.

Mindy, Bertie, and Melinda leap up, but all they can do is watch in helpless frustration. The main caravan moves out of the camp and the collegiates watch in horror as Bonny and her guard slip away in the machine-gun cart. As one, they wave and shout, "Bonny, we love you. Be strong." They mumble among themselves, wipe away tears, and continue waving at the fading caravan.

Bonny shouts to her friends and sends a halfhearted wave. Now, the stark reality of their unknown fate as prisoners of Chinese bandits grips the collegiates with harrowing apprehension.

The thoughts running through their minds include *Where are we going? How long is this march? What will these bandits do to us? Rape? Slavery? Torture? Death? Will the authorities rescue us? What will happen to us? Will we ever return home?*

Sergeant Hsu Su-en settles one of the questions in short order. He compels the prisoners to a forced march at gunpoint. Without proper footwear, the march is a nightmare. Maureen and Randolph have a particularly difficult time. As the terrain's elevation increases, the cooler it becomes—approximately two degrees Centigrade per one thousand feet. At the end of the day, the hostages are debilitated from lack of food and water, and their feet are swollen and painful. The guards refuse to build a campfire for fear of being spotted by the pursuing forces. The prisoners are not dressed for the cooler temperatures, do not have blankets, and suffer accordingly. They huddle for mutual warmth.

Mindy, by default, becomes the leader of the remaining collegiates. She sits on the ground and rubs her bare feet; she says with a tinge of humor, "Now tell me, what the hell sort of a moving picture will this bandit episode make? It matters not. Include me out."

Bertie and Melinda smile feebly at Mindy's humor. Melinda comments weakly, "Let's find someone else to take my part, I'm a terrible actress."

Bertie flops and says, "Ditto. No pictures for me." She pantomimes with her hand and lips, and asks, "When the hell do we eat? I'm wolfishly hungry."

The others chime, "Ditto" and "Amen."

Randolph rubs Maureen's feet. "Hang tough, dear. We'll make it," he says, though internally he is not so confident.

Perhaps because of the language barrier, the Chinese hostages keep to themselves. The older fellow is wheezing, and appears to be exhausted.

Later, a bandit brings food to the hostages for their first meal of the day—one raw potato, and a strip of hardtack for each. He offers a small jug with just enough water for one healthy swallow each.

Maureen knows that she must hide her heirloom jewelry if she has any chance of keeping it. *After this fiasco is over, there is the possibility that I or Dolph can return to retrieve it,* she concludes. She spots a large, diamond-shaped volcanic rock in a small copse of pine trees. Later, when the guards snore and the collegiates are asleep, she urges Randolph to explore the rock. He finds a large, deep crack and stuffs her jewelry far down into it. He then covers the crack with small rocks and sod. On the back of the rock, he makes random scratches to aid in finding it later.

地陰

The next day, the prisoners trek for miles through high grass strewn with running streams and volcanic rocks. Mindy stumbles in stagnant water and falls into mud. A guard pulls her erect and threatens her with a pistol to the back of her head because she is not keeping the pace.

Later in the morning, the troop reach the crest of the hill. Below lies a valley with planted crops of rice and maze. In the distance are the rocky Patu-ku Mountains.

The older Chinese baggage-car porter is exhausted and collapses in the deep moist grass. One of the guards beats him fiercely, demanding that he stand and keep moving. His face is drained white. He looks at the guard with pleading eyes that say, *I do not have the strength or will to rise and continue.* The bandit guard screams wildly, and then fires his Mauser until the porter's body no longer twitches.

Maureen screams and begins talking loudly to no one in particular. Randolph wraps his arms around his wife and whispers, "Quiet, dear. That fellow obviously does not understand English and he might assume that we are plotting an escape."

The collegiates turn away as if not seeing the horrible scene means it does not exist.

With uncontrollable anger, the younger porter grabs a rock, leaps at the killer guard, and yells at him in Mandarin, "You killed my uncle."

Before the guard can reload, the porter smashes the rock into the side of the guard's head. The fellow slides to the ground, mortally wounded. Captain Chao fires a full clip from his Mauser into the porter and he falls without life. Chao spouts, "Peasant, you had no value. My soldier did."

The hostages drop to the ground to avoid stray bullets. Randolph covers his wife.

Bertie cries out, "I can't stand any more of this torment and horror. I am going to run away." She rises on one knee.

Mindy tackles her. "No, you won't. They'll kill you or something worse." Mindy grabs Bertie in a bear hug and they bawl in deep wailing sobs.

Melinda demands, "Stop it! Get up. The guards want us to move away from here. Now!"

As the prisoners trudge along, no one dares to speak. Each wonders if he or she is destined for a similar fate. Several hours later, Maureen whispers to Randolph, "We are in the hands of desperate blackguards. What is your assessment?"

"I've no idea, dear. Our goal is to survive. Pay whatever ransom these bandits demand, return to the good ol' USA, and continue our lives."

池阝彐

Several hours later, Sergeant Hsu guides the troops to the nearby village of Tsaochwang. The population gathers to see the Occidentals, a unique experience for the vast majority. Children rush to see and touch the white people. A few light firecrackers in welcome. Others offer water and rice cakes to the hostages. Melinda eagerly takes a large bite, and then coughs and coughs. She gulps her water. She whispers to Bertie, "Is this fried paper?"

"Who knows?" responds Bertie. "At my stage of starvation, I'll eat almost anything."

Captain Chao orders a halt and indicates that the troop will spend the night here. The prisoners drop to the dirt street and tackle the cakes and water.

Melinda finishes first, holds her empty cup up to Sergeant Hsu, and asks, "More?"

Her body motion is more communicative than her words, Hsu knows the consequences if they do not deliver all the prisoners in reasonably fine condition. Sun will not care about the dead Chinese porters. Chao talks to a teenage lad in the crowd. The boy dashes to the village well, draws a bucket of water, and brings it to Chao. Satisfied, he hands the bucket to Randolph and indicates that he is to share the water with all.

Bertie gulps several swallows and says, "Damn, that was good." She drinks more, and looks at the water in the bucket. *I wonder how many horrible diseases are in this water? Who cares?* She drinks her fill—as do the rest.

The village elders arrive and assess the scene. The senior elder expresses concern at the obviously poor condition of the prisoners. He issues orders to those about. "Take these people to the shrine, offer them proper food and blankets, and summon the *Yishi* to tend to their wounds." Captain Chao protests loudly. The elder waves him away. Chao knows he dare not make an issue with the elder—a confidant of bandit Sun.

Stout fellows bring five rickshaws. The collegiates climb aboard.

Bertie asks, "What now?" She wiggles comfortably in the soft cushions. "Who cares? I feel better already."

Randolph, with tender care, helps his wife into one of the conveyances. "At last, dear, we are in civilization and it appears that that fellow in charge is going to take care of us."

Maureen slides into the rickshaw. She is near the end of her endurance. "Let's hope so, Dolph," she says. "I cannot travel much farther."

He gently pats her on the arm. "I know, dear. I'll look out for you."

On the elder's signal, his fellows pick up the rickshaws' harnesses and begin to trot to the shine. The collegiates spot an attractive Chinese woman standing in the doorway of a shop of some sort. She is dressed in bright red silks and wears an ivory broach at her neck. She realizes that the hostages are from the Shanghai Express, strikes a model's pose, and twirls around; she is anxious to announce her new station and to display her jewelry.

Mindy comments, "I recognize her. She is one of Fu's concubines. I saw that broach on that Italian woman—obviously it's loot from the train. Is Fu here?" she asks rhetorically.

"No, of course not. Fu is too important a mandarin to be in this god-forsaken outpost of civilization," Melinda responds. With a touch of sarcasm, she continues, "No doubt he's in his palace in Peiping, luxuriating in a warm bath tinted with aromatic bath salts, sipping century-old champagne, a professional masseuse rubbing his back, and scantily clad women tending to his pleasures."

Partially satiated, the collegiates laugh heartily at Melinda's scene.

Mindy quips, "Obviously, this concubine has been sold to someone—a rice merchant in the village probably. Where's the other?"

Melinda snaps, "Who cares?"

The Occidentals fail to notice that Captain Chao and his squad are trotting behind the rickshaws.

At the shrine, they enjoy the village's best hospitality. The meals consist of a mush of rice, kernels of maize, and a few thin slices of pork. "Delicious," is the universal appraisal. The *Yìshī* tends to their abrasions; his female aides massage swollen feet and bring slippers for all. That night, inside the shrine's covered porch, the Occidentals sleep on straw mattresses covered with blankets.

Around midnight, the corporal of the rear guard arrives, gives a snappy salute to Captain Chao, and reports, "Sir, mysteriously the pursuing militia and soldiers have returned to Lincheng. I know not why."

"At ease, Corporal. Good news, no doubt. Probably orders from higher military authorities." Captain Chao smiles inwardly, suspecting the reason for the return.

At sunrise, Sergeant Hsu rousts the Occidentals and soon has them moving through a wide plain spread before the steep-faced Patu-ku Mountains. At mid-morning, they climb dozens of steep stairs cut in solid rock. Maureen stumbles several times, but Randolph catches her, and they continue. Near the summit, the trail opens to a large, verdant valley. At the far end is an ancient temple, which the bandits have converted to Sun's elegant headquarters.

1Ø

Bandit Sun's Hideaway, Patu-ku Mountains, Shantung Province.
Noon, 7–9 May 1923

The exhausted prisoners enter Sun's hideaway compound and spot Bonny standing in the doorway of a sprawling rock structure. She waves to them. She is dressed in a fine blue silk Ruqun ensemble with red collar and sash, a style from the Jin Dynasty. Her hair is cut professionally and cascades to her shoulders in smooth folds; her cheeks are rosy; and her lips have a faint touch of rouge.

Rousing their last reserve, her friends rush to her and grab her in bear hugs. Kisses are exchanged all around. Sweet tears of joy flow on their cheeks. They all try to talk at once, communicating that they are tired, well, delirious to see that Bonny is okay, and relieved that their debilitating journey is ended for now.

The girls ask about Bonny's apparently excellent condition and her fine gown in this infernal place.

Bonny responds, "Sun's first wife, the head woman 'round here, the *Qizi*, is a tough and demanding ol' bird. She rules this compound with an iron fist. On my first day here, much to my regret, I learned quickly to do exactly as she demands—do it quickly and with skill, else you'll feel her wrath. No foolin.'" Reflexively, she rubs her face and *derrière* as testament to her words. "On the other hand, she apparently has instructions from Sun to ensure that we look presentable and are treated reasonably well. It has to do with the ransoms or something."

Bonny steps back, looks at her friends, and asks in a sober voice, "Hey, any news about Thea—that good-lookin' Tejana?"

The collegiates cast their eyes downward. Mindy says somberly, "We have no more information about Thea. Clearly, she was seriously wounded, maybe even killed. We don't know."

Bonny cries, "My God! My friend Thea. These ruthless yellow bandits are spawns of the Devil. We pray that she's alive, that she was rescued and recovers."

Each expresses agreement: "Amen." "Indeed." "And how." "Absolutely."

Bonny pulls a handkerchief from one of her flowing sleeves and wipes a tear. "How foolish we were to imagine that capture by these Chinese bandits would be some romantic adventure." With flashing eyes she exclaims, "If we survive, there's no damn moving picture for us."

Sergeant Hsu, with a thrust of his rifle, herds the Occidentals to the main house, where the *Qizi* is waiting for them. She clearly is irritated that she had to wait for them. She immediately takes firm control of the Occidentals by slapping each on the left cheek, including Randolph and Maureen.

Through a young woman interpreter, a Christian convert named Sue Chen, the *Qizi* explains the rules of their captivity and of the compound. "I am Sun's first wife. I rule this household. Strictly obey my orders—else you will suffer severe punishment."

She assigns the Van Halsteds a small apartment with a double bed. To the collegiates, she assigns two Spartan, but sufficient, rooms.

"You will work in this compound as all of us do. You eat twice a day in your rooms." She squints her eyes, further enhancing her wrinkled face. "Stay in, or near, this area and no one will bother you. Behave and be content until ransomed. Understand?" Without waiting for an answer, she hobbles into her quarters on bound feet. Sue Chen follows. She glances back and flashes a wistful smile.

池陣

A couple of days after their arrival, Sun orders the hostages to write letters to their families. He speaks through Sue Chen. "Tell them about the excellent treatment Sun and his cadre are providing. Talk about your comfortable living environment and how you spend the day. Praise the delicious meals. When you have completed your letters, hand them to Sue Chen. She will read them to ensure that they meet my standards."

Sue gives a slight bow.

Sun continues, "Also, each of you will write letters to President Warren Harding and the British Prime Minister Sir Stanley Baldwin, pleading for them not to try to rescue you from Sun's impregnable fortress because, should anyone try, the bandit Sun surely will execute you. Shortly, he will send ransom demands through an intermediary." He looks carefully at each hostage and continues, "I expect you to complete this task before the evening meal and to write each letter correctly." He cracks a forced smile. "If not, you will have to rewrite your letters under less than favorable conditions."

Chen waits until Sun has gone. She addresses the hostages. "I also am a hostage—captured from a Lutheran mission in Supeh Province many years ago. I have no one to pay my ransom. I shall die here, earning my keep by translating for the bandit and his *Qizi*: English, Japanese, Russian, and French. Anyway, no one in this compound can read or speak English. Write as Sun directed, but in the subtext, let your parents and officials know that your letter is a charade. I will approve all the letters."

Later, Sun sends Sergeant Hsu Su-en to the German Catholic mission at Chefoo in Shantung Province. Hsu's task is to deliver the Occidentals' letters to the German post office, and to invite Father Viktor Max Lenfers to visit Sun's fortress with news of the outside world. Occasionally, the *priester* had done similar work for Sun's other prisoners. Father Lenfers had moved to China in the late 19th century and settled in Shantung Province, then part of the German Colonial Empire, as allowed in the extraterritorial treaty signed in the 1850s.

Within the next two days, deserters from other gangs and warlord armies join Sun's brigands. They defect to Sun's flag because of his bold attack on the hated Occidentals, who had imposed unequal treaties, and for the opportunity to share in future raids and loot. Under Sergeant Tang Tse-che's strict discipline and training, most become effective fighting men. The others are shot for learning too much about Sun's operations.

Concurrently, Father Lenfers arrives with a donkey loaded with canned goods, sausages, fresh fruits, rye bread, fruit jams, chocolates, and a dozen copies of the English-language newspaper, *The Shanghai Times*. The priester is a powerful-looking man, almost sixty years old, with a hooked, chiseled nose, a mane of grey hair, and bright blue eyes.

Sun greets him heartily. "Welcome, my old friend. I'm delighted to see you again after all these months." He motions to the goods on the donkey. "You have my word, *priester*, that your provisions are only for the hostages." He hands Father Lenfers a British five hundred pound sterling note. With a mocking voice, Sun says, "This is genuine coin of the realm and will cover your expenses, not so?"

Father Lenfers responds softly, "I'm loath to accept blood money from you, bandit Sun, but our mission is desperate in the chaos that engulfs this province. I look away as you make a donation in my basket." He turns and tells Sun, "I will see if I can offer solace to the hostages. Perhaps one is Catholic; if so, I shall hear confession and administer communion."

"Indeed, you shall."

"The meetings between the hostages and me are private and we will not discuss them. *Verstehen*, bandit?"

"Yes. Yes. Get on with it. We have serious business to discuss."

A couple of hours later, Father Lenfers expresses his outrage to Sun over the Shanghai Express incident and the murder and kidnapping of the Occidentals. In his sternest voice, Father Lenfers says, "Bandit Sun, I abhor your criminal conduct. You are evil personified. I wonder if you are possessed with a demon." He removes his crucifix from the wide brown belt around his cassock and uses it to make the sign of the cross over Sun. In a futile gesture, he demands in Latin, "*Váde retro sátana*." Again, he makes the sign of the cross. "In the name of the Holy Trinity, Satan, be gone. Quit thee to hell!" Knowing that it is useless, he shakes his head. "Sun, I should leave and let Lucifer steal what soul you have."

Sun laughs hilariously. "*Priester*, you speak of souls and devils. There are no such specters." He pats Lenfers gently on the back. "There are only glittering plunder, nubile women, and the good life of pleasure." He roars in mocking laughter. "Debauchery, you call it."

Father Lenfers shouts, "A pox on your house. I go." He swats the donkey on the rump and starts to move away.

"Wait, please, *priester,* I would ask a favor of you." Sun speaks in an earnest voice.

"What evil do you want from me?"

"A simple request, my old friend. As my representative, go to the British Red Cross in Shanghai, and ask them to appoint a negotiator to mediate my ransom demands and make the arrangements for the exchange of the hostages."

"I've no time for such piratical business, bandit. I have integrity and will not represent the sins in your soul in any endeavor. Take care of such dealings yourself." He takes a few steps forward.

Sun grabs him and with malice says, "You know very well, I cannot leave here. I am a prisoner in my own prison. Even now, my scouts tell me that the Occidentals are making preparations to rescue my hostages." More calmly he asks, "Where is your compassion for the souls of my hostages? If you fail me, you shall say a Requiem Mass for them."

Shocked at Sun's threat, Father Lenfers mulls over an appropriate response. But he is at a loss. *I cannot be a party to banditry, nor can I cause the death of the Occidentals.*

Sun says in his most consoling voice, "Father Lenfers, your dilemma is so clear. Let me help you decide." He signals to Captain Chao Tan-keng.

Captain Chao approaches, leading a donkey with a bulging saddlebag on each side. Sun slaps one of the saddlebags and the tinkle of coins emanates. "Would five thousand Mexican silver pesos be a sufficient inducement to soothe your conscience?"

Angrily, Father Lenfers shouts, "Damn you, bandit Sun Mei-yao. You tempt me with pieces of silver. You are a demon!" Lenfers drops to the ground on his knees, makes the sign of the cross, and shouts, "Am I to hang myself on an olive tree?"

"Nonsense, my old friend. Let me help you rise." After Lenfers is standing, Sun hands him the donkey's guide rope.

Father Lenfers looks at him with downcast eyes and begins to walk toward that narrow cut in the granite mountain, leading both donkeys behind him.

Sun shouts mockingly, "*Bon voyage.*"

11

Various locations around the world.
9–10 May 1923

The wireless telegraphs hum with vivid accounts of the bandit Sun Mei-yao's ambush, the destruction of the elite British Shanghai Express railroad train, and the heinous atrocities inflicted on the Occidental passengers. Newspapers worldwide publish story after story of the catastrophe, supplemented with wire photographs of the wreckage and litter. There are no comments from the two surviving women.

For reasons not stated, the British government has not made any enquiries about the disappearance of his Majesty's subject Madam Margaret Jasperson, a travel agent working for American Express out of Peiping.

Agents for the U.S. State Department's Bureau of Intelligence and Research and the British Secret Intelligence Service (MI6) have cordoned off the recovering Laura and Thea from relatives, the press, and any other visitors. Only cleared medical personnel are allowed anywhere near them. The agents debrief the patients in small bits that increase in intensity as the women slowly recover. Thea's jaw is wired shut. She writes her responses.

The tabloid publications scream of the "yellow man's" treachery: murders, rapine, and kidnappings. Such chronicles engender severe reactions from the public and officials in the United States, Great Britain, France, and Italy on behalf of their respective citizens who were victims of Sun's raid. Enraged by such brazen effrontery in the face of their extraterritorial treaty rights in China, the foreign powers discuss the formation of a unified military command to rescue the hostages and destroy Sun and his bandit gang.

他處.

From Nanking, Sun Yat-sen, Generalissimo of the Military Government of Central China, sends his sends his deepest apologies to the affected Western governments for Sun Mei-yao's horrendous barbarity. Universally, the Occidental leaders understand that China's weak Nationalist government does not have the will or capability to contribute military forces. Sun Yat-sen's limited resources are fighting warlords and banditry, and trying to extend the Kuomintang's control of northern and southern China.

他處.

Via a transatlantic cable, the Secretary of State for the United States, Charles Evan Hughes; Foreign Secretary of Great Britain, Marques George Curzon; the Italian Minister for Foreign Affairs, Dino Grandi; and Raymond Poincare, President of the French Council and Minister for Foreign Affairs hold daily conferences discussing what grand strategy they need to rescue the hostages. The ministers conclude that their missing citizens probably are hostages of the bandit Sun Mei-yao. After numerous cable conferences, they decide that because the Shanghai Express is a British enterprise, Great Britain should take the lead in countering this international incident.

The next day, the British Prime Minister Sir Stanley Baldwin appoints Lieutenant General Heathcliff Percival-Trengove, GC, DSO, the commanding officer of an international brigade. His assignment is to rescue Sun's hostages and to dispatch the bandit and his gang. He is an old China hand. During the siege of Peking in the Boxer Rebellion of 1900, Sub-Lieutenant Percival-Trengove was a inside the wall of the foreign legation compound and fought with exceptional bravery. Currently, he is the commandant of British forces in Southeast Asia, with headquarters in Singapore.

The head of the Secret Intelligence Service (MI6), Captain Sir Mansfield George Smith-Cumming, KCMB, CG, tasks his agents in the Far East with assisting Lieutenant General Percival-Trengove in full measure.

他走.

British Prime Minister Baldwin stands before Parliament at Question Time. Member Ramsay MacDonald, Labor Party, demands, "Would the Minister justify another military action in China? The loss of the Shanghai Express is regretful, but not an act of war. I see no exceptional reason to instigate another fight in the Far East. We have wasted too many of our young men in lost causes. When is enough enough?"

Baldwin responds, "Honorable Member from Oldham East, our army is the spearhead of Great Britain. Our soldiers' lost lives are regrettable. Nonetheless, our men fight in foreign lands to protect our Empire." He pauses and scans the chamber and gallery. Seeing that he has made his point, he continues, "The monetary damage to the Shanghai Express is high, perhaps one million pounds, including indemnities. Of more significance, the bandits murdered two of our finest citizens—a major in the Royal Marines and his courageous wife—and a number of other Occidentals from civilized nations. It's murder, rape, kidnapping, and plunder that threatens our Empire. We dare not let these injustices expire without severe retaliation. Our prestige will suffer highly. The savages will consider our cowardice *carte blanche* to wage further atrocities. What will happen to our Crown Colony Hong Kong and the New Territories? Our position in the International Settlement in Shanghai, and all of the Extra Territorial ports and cities we administer in China? I dare not consider the consequences if we do not act, act aggressively, and act now."

The members shout a rousing "Hear! Hear! Hear!" in war fever.

Clearly defeated, MacDonald mumbles, "I yield."

Baldwin says, "Thank you Honorable Member. Let's pray that we need not have to resort to the military option. I have a cable from our *attaché* in Peiping, Commander Stanhope-Owston. He reports that our diplomatic officials are working with our Red Cross in Shanghai to develop a negotiating team to deal with the bandit Sun Mei-yao, find his ransom terms, and make arrangements for the hostage exchange." His tone and volume rise. "I must say, however, we will not condone the payment of ransom—it's blackmail, pure and simple. Such chicanery will only encourage the blackguards to commit further atrocities on our subjects and enterprises in the Far East. My instructions to the War Office are to negotiate first for the release of the Occidentals. If that fails, use the force of arms to rescue them."

There is another rousing, "Hear! Hear! Hear!" from the chamber.

Member MacDonald slumps in his chair and sadly wonders, *Where does this spilling of British blood end? Have we not had enough? Gallipoli, Passchendaele, the Somme, Balochisten, the Boer Campaign, the Sudan?* He tries to hide his tears, but cannot.

12

MI6 Spaces, British Legation Basement, International Settlement, Shanghai. 1000 hours, 11–14 May 1923

"Stop! I have *no* more to say. I wash my hands of this dubious business," Father Lenfers demands.

Chief of Station, Secret Intelligence Service Agent Cholmondeley Alastair says, "Father Lenfers, we thank you for your excellent cooperation. The names of Sun's hostages and the other information you've provided are critically important and will facilitate their rescue." He withdraws a sheet from his valise. "*Priester*, according to King's Regulations, I must classify your report Confidential. With your signature on this Official Secrets Act document we will conclude our business. Again, you've been a great help."

Father Lenfers signs and mumbles something that resembles, "Thank you." Under his breath he says, "These stuffed-shirt British will force the Devil to sign documents to let them enjoy his hospitality."

"Yes, *Priester*? You said ...?"

"Nothing. Talking with myself."

Lenfers moves outside and hails a rickshaw. He looks across the street and spots the large Red Cross sign atop the building. Guilt grips him. He makes the sign of the cross. *Dear God, I've betrayed the bandit Sun Mei-yao to British Intelligence, forgive my sin of duplicity and my acceptance of his silver coins with false intent. Our mission is poor and our want is great. Amen.*

池嵘

MI6 agent Alastair briefs the British military *attaché*, Commander James Stanhope-Owston, DFC, MC, on the details of Father Lenfer's information: the layout of Sun's compound, order of battle, fortifications, and firing positions in the mountains. "The *priester* was adamant that Sun holds only six hostages, all Occidentals. He has talked with each one, and he has given us their names. All are in fine physical condition—though they are disconcerted at their imprisonment and the threat of death extant."

Stanhope-Owston comments, "Well done. Perhaps we can use the *priester* again as a sub rosa agent."

"Not likely. He has no love for the British. He lost his brother at Jutland in the Great War."

"Very well. Brief me on these Occidental hostages."

Alastair refreshes his memory with the names scribbled in his notebook. "They are Randolph Van Halsted, his wife Maureen, and four college girls—Mindy Whitestone, Bertie Campbell, Bonny Baker, and Melinda Callahan." He ruffles through his notes. "Sun's men killed two Chinese porters, names unknown, during the trek to his hideout."

Stanhope-Owston says, "Very well. Who was killed during the raid?"

Alastair flips more pages in his notebook. "Inside the train, we found the bodies of four first-class Occidental passengers and one Eurasian female—apparently all murdered during the ambush: British Royal Marine Major Quinten Ashley-Cooper and his wife Karina; the American missionary, Doctor Todd Fleet; the Italian businessman, Nani Atticus; and the Eurasian café owner, Mae Ling-weh."

"That's all? Where are the rest?" Stanhope-Owston checks his passenger list. "I reckon there ought to be six more first-class passengers and the porter. Where are they?"

Alastair frets internally, *There are only five passengers missing.* Feeling somewhat chagrined, Alastair responds, "We do not know. What happened to the remaining passengers is an unfathomable mystery. We've searched the area for several miles around the wreck and have found nothing." He closes his eyes as if in deep thought. "It's possible that the rising river could have washed away a body or two."

Stanhope-Owston stares at Alastair with questioning eyes. He knows that the Secret Intelligence Service agent is lying and says, "Who are these missing people?"

Alastair flips open his *attaché* case, withdraws a couple of pages, and says, "Here they are." He hands the list of names and a brief dossier on each of the missing passengers to Stanhope-Owston.

Stanhope-Owston studies the list. "I see that you've tagged the White Russian, Stephan Paskhim, as a possible agent for Japan's Black Dragon Society. Confirmed?"

"We don't know much about Paskhim except that he's some sort of a vicious international rogue and has frequent contact with unsavory Japanese civilians."

"What about the French cinema actress Monique Harmonie? She seems harmless enough."

Alastair responds, "Perhaps. She is a *colon* from Dà Nàng in French Indo-China. We've no clue why she is unaccounted for. It's most peculiar." He pauses to gather his thoughts. "There is a faint whiff of intelligence that she had other interests, as yet unknown."

Alastair continues, "Here's a poser. Still uncounted for is Xenia De Luca. She was the traveling companion of Nani Atticus, an industrialist on the run from the Italian secret police for stealing highly classified military plans who was reportedly carrying a large measure of cash. We have limited information about De Luca. Apparently, she is a posh prostitute who worked the Italian Riviera. Atticus' cash and plans are missing. We do not know if she killed him or a stray bandit bullet did. Enquiries are continuing."

Stanhope-Owston cracks a large smile. "You cloak-and-dagger fellows practice a strange art with even stranger characters. Who's this Bridget von Cairo?"

Alastair smiles faintly. "She is best described as an international adventuress. She has no known nationality, is of indefinite age, and has several passports, including one from the Vatican. INTERPOL informs us that they have a warrant for her arrest for some sort of art fraud perpetrated in San Francisco by an international criminal gang operating out of Istanbul."

"Amazing. And this was supposed to be a routine run for the Shanghai Express so that the elite Occidentals could mix and match. What a tangled web you fellows weave."

Ignoring the friendly jibe, Alastair continues, "Most curious is that the steward, Mahima Rahman, is missing as well. He's been with the Shanghai Express since it started service last year. His quarterly reports in efficiency and courtesy are stellar. His supervisor spoke highly of him."

"Any clues?"

"None whatsoever."

Stanhope-Owston rubs his chin and scratches where it does not itch. "Something really bizarre occurred on that train in the few hours before the ambush. Got a guess?"

Alastair frowns and slowly shakes his head no. "I've none. It's as if a *deus ex machina* descended on these people and had its Greek way with them. We just do not know." He muses, *I'm going to have a long talk with Margaret Jasperson.*

Alastair continues his litany, "The last character in this scenario is the Chinese gangster and opium lord, Fu Kuang-hsŭ. Yesterday, we spotted him in his 'secret' lair in Peiping, conducting his illicit business as usual." He closes his journal, places it in his valise, and checks his watch. *It's 1630 hours. That's enough for today.* "Commander, let's adjourn to a pub I know. It's full of beautiful ladies from the International Settlement." He dons his bowler and starts towards the door. "If that does not suit you, we'll journey to a café in the French Concession where the *dames* are just so *oo la la. D'accord?*"

Stanhope-Owston cocks his head slightly and says, "I see from the train's passenger list that there was a Margaret Jasperson, an English woman, among the passengers. What do you know of her?"

Alastair snaps, "We know of no such person."

"Mister Alastair, are you joshing me? Margaret Jasperson is the name on the manifest."

"Commander, that list must be in error. There was no one on board the Shanghai Express with that name."

Commander Stanhope-Owston understands Alastair's protestations. "Very well. Obviously the passenger list was in error." He puts on his cap and says, "Let's go."

At the same moment, Margaret Jasperson is being debriefed by an MI6 agent in a safe house in Chefoo. The Secret Intelligence Service fellow is only slightly annoyed that Jasperson killed the *Deuxième Bureau* agent Monique Harmonie. He rationalizes, *Why not? Tit for tat.*

地陪

The next morning, in the conference room of the Red Cross building, Commander Stanhope-Owston discusses a sanitized version of the *priester's* report with a clique that includes embassy representatives from the affected countries, medical personnel, and Red Cross executives. He adds background information on Sun Mei-yao and his brigands from Scotland Yard's Shanghai Branch *dossier,* which includes Sun's record at the Whampoa Military Academy and apocryphal data from various sources.

The Commander continues, "This morning, our task is to tag a trusted British subject to negotiate with the bandit Sun Mei-yao for the release of his hostages." He looks about the room and nods to the head of the Red Cross in China, Mister Carl Crow.

Crow does not hesitate. He announces, "Gentlemen, based on the information presented today, I would suggest that Major Sir John Starly, Secretary of the Red Cross, is the logical choice to negotiate with the bandit Sun. He is fluent in Mandarin and, over his years in China, he has come to understand Chinese personal customs and business protocols. He has an excellent reputation among the local population for his empathetic mien and straightforward dealings."

John Starly stands and says in a too-loud voice, with a tinge of protest, "I know nothing of banditry or how to negotiate with Chinese marauders. Choose someone else who is qualified." He is a slim, tall fellow with deep brown eyes and a strong, square chin. Wounded at Passchendaele in 1917, ex-Major Starly walks with a heavy limp and uses an ebony cane with a silver lion's head. "For the sake of the hostages, I must decline your invitation. I would muck it up," he says with finality.

Carl Crow addresses Starly, "John, you underestimate your skills. I know you will perform superlatively. You have the courage and industry to complete this task."

Commander Stanhope-Owston interjects, "Once again, Major Starly—for King and Country."

Starly stands and swings his cane around the room, ensuring that his gesture encompasses all who hector him. "You try my soul, gentlemen. You make no cogent argument except that I have no option." He taps his cane hard on the wood floor several times, and the *click, click, click* reverberates around the room. He pauses to calm himself and sits. "Accordingly, I accept your commission."

Shouts of "Jolly good, ol' man!" "*Félicitations à vou!*" "Congratulations!" and "*Complimenti!*" ring out from those present.

Starly, still slightly irritated, responds, "Yes. Yes. Yes. Let's get on with it—whatever *it* might be."

Commander Stanhope-Owston escorts Starly into an anteroom, instructs him on the conventions of acting as a representative of His Majesty's Government, and briefs him on Father Lenfers' information regarding Sun's egomania, the hostages, and the layout of his compound. As they prepare to leave, the commander tells Starly, "Major, I must have your signature on this Official Secrets Act document."

Flustered by this last bit of bureaucracy, Starly says too softly, "Yes. Of course." He signs, and hands the paper to the commander. "I'm not thrilled with this assignment, but I'll carry on to full measure."

Commander Stanhope-Owston sends a telegram to the railroad agent in Chefoo for delivery to Sun Mei-yao's representative:

MISTER JOHN STARLY OF THE BRITISH RED CROSS REPRESENTS HIS BRITANNIC MAJESTY'S GOVERNMENT STOP HE IS VEST-ED WITH PLENIPOTENTIARY AUTHORITY TO

NEGOTIATE FOR RELEASE OF THE OCCIDENTAL
HOSTAGES YOU HOLD FROM THE RAID ON THE
SHANGHAI EXPRESS STOP HE COMES TO THE
PATU-KU MOUNTAINS WITH A WHITE FLAG
OF TRUCE STOP YOU ARE ENJOINED BY
ALL RULES OF INTERNATIONAL CONDUCT TO
HONOR THIS CONVENTION STOP COMMANDER
JAMES STANHOPE-OWSTON MILITARY ATTACHÉ
LEGATION PEIPING

池時

Starly begins to assemble a crew and equipment for the trek to Sun's hide-out. He gathers food, clothing, medical supplies, letters from home for the hostages, and several pounds of Johnson Candy's chocolates—including several boxes of the delicious turtles. Two days later, he, his crew, and the supplies are on board the light cruiser *HMS Diomede* en route at high speed to the Japanese naval base at Tsingtao. From there, Japanese marines will truck the crew to the base of the Patu-ku Mountains.

When Starly and his porters arrive at the base of the mountain, Sergeant Tang and his squad are waiting for him. Tang speaks in Mandarin, "Mister Starly, we will carry the supplies and escort you and one of your porters to our headquarters."

Starly looks about to get his bearings and responds, "Very well." He charges the remaining porter to standby. "God willing, I'll return later this afternoon."

池處.

Sun greets Starly in the grand teahouse with a hearty handshake and a pat on the back. "Welcome to my compound, Mister Starly of the British Red Cross. Or is it Major John Starly of the British Expeditionary Force in Belgium?" He laughs heartily. "You see, Major Starly, I have my own intelligence service—I'm not an illiterate barbarian." He struts about briefly. "I am an honors graduate of the Whampoa Military Academy. You are surprised?"

Starly, unsure of the protocol in this instance, responds flatly, "No. I know your background. Let's get on with our business."

Sun motions to Sergeant Tang. "Please excuse me, but we must search you to ensure that you do not have a weapon, a camera to gather intelligence, or secret messages for my prisoners—perhaps about an escape plan. Is that not so?"

"Do I have a choice, bandit Sun?" replies Starly.

"Unfortunately not. Either a search or a pistol to your head."

"Your hospitality lacks finesse."

Sergeant Tang conducts the search with deft skills. He makes a negative shake of his head. He proceeds to search the porter—again, with negative results.

Sun, with a forced smile, says, "Join me in a toast to convivial dealings. I have an excellent Napoleon brandy—somehow lost from the French Concession in Shanghai."

"Not now, Sun. Let's conclude our business and I shall depart with your demands. Or, perhaps, with the hostages?"

With a cocked eye, Sun says in a faux hurtful voice, "You reject my hospitality and make unreasonable assumptions. Such actions do not bode well for convivial and productive negotiations. It is too late this afternoon to conclude our business." He signals to the main house. "You will spend the night here and we shall talk tomorrow morning." A courtesan walks in erotic syncopation toward the pair. Sun nods to the woman. With a pleasant smile, she moves to Starly and attempts to take his hand.

He pulls it away quickly. "No, Sun." With a tight jaw and narrow eyes, he responds, "Let us conclude our business now. First, I should want to talk with the hostages. Then, tell me your hostage demands, and I will leave."

"Unfortunately, I must insist that you stay." A smile creeps over Sun face. "We have much to discuss, and I do not want to be hurried. Surely you understand."

"I do *not* understand. What are your terms for the hostages?"

With a touch of anger, Sun fires, "You will spend the night as my guest."

Starly realizes that to pursue his preference any further would jeopardize his mission. He responds, "If you insist, I'll defer."

"I do insist, Major British Red Cross."

"Very well. Show me to my quarters and where I shall dine. The same for my porter, if you please. Now, I would like to visit with your prisoners and distribute the letters and parcels I've brought."

Sun snaps, "My guests are unavailable to you. Such a meeting is not on my agenda." He pours a tall drink of the brandy and takes a deep swallow. His eyes narrow. "You will stay in the guest house. My men and I thank you sincerely for the thoughtfulness of bringing these parcels of British goods and the chocolate turtles. We will dine well this evening." He laughs at his duplicity, and at the look of shock and disgust on Starly's face. "The letters I shall hold to ensure good behavior from my hostages."

"Sun! Indeed, you are a blackguard. How can the British trust you?"

Still laughing, Sun manages to say, "They cannot."

Starly, shocked at this betrayal of honorable dealings, stammers, "You have no honor, Sun. Shortly, you will face the imperial might of His Majesty's government, and you and your entire gang will depart violently this Celestial Kingdom."

"Such bravado. I am impressed." He begins to laugh almost uncontrollably at the stupid Englishman. Soon, he recovers and announces, "Mister Red Cross, Major John Starly, I have been remiss. I have failed to inform you that as of now, you are my prisoner." His sardonic laughter returns. "I need one of His Majesty's subjects for my hostage—an official who will bring a large ransom from the British government." His laughter continues at his clever lure of Starly to his compound under a false flag.

Starly stands as tall and as erect as he can, points his cane at the bandit, and in his most imperious voice says, "Sun Mei-yao, you are a dead man waiting to happen."

"It is so. My honorable ancestors have waited for me for some time."

Starly, staring into Sun's dark eyes, presses a hidden button in the cane's silver handle. The escaping carbon dioxide explodes in a white cloud and catapults the cover of his cane skyward, revealing a rapier. Starly lunges for Sun with a quick *coup de point.* He misses.

Sun is quicker. He knew it was a sword cane as soon as he heard the hiss of the escaping gas; he fell away.

Sergeant Tang stuns Starly with a blow to the head from the butt of his pistol and the Major falls to the ground.

"Sergeant Tang, help Major Starly upright and bring him before me. Well, Major Starly, I congratulate you on your imagination and courage— to no avail, I'm delighted to say. What shall I do with you for this betrayal of your white flag of truce—a betrayal of your British trust? A flogging? How about a crucifixion? Shall we defer to your rank and settle for a simple firing squad? What say you, Major?"

Starly, chagrined that he has failed and betrayed his honor, stands as close to attention as he can, stares at Sun with defiant eyes, and remains mute.

After a time, Sun says, "Very well, Major." He starts to laugh, hysterically. Through his guffaws, he manages to say, "You Britons, so noble. So clumsy. So treacherous. You are of my kind. No, I shall keep you for the ransom." He recovers his composure. "Sergeant Tang, escort Major Starly to the guest house. No need to lock it. Major, should you make any untoward moves, I will kill a hostage." Mockingly, he lashes out, "Do you understand, Maah-jur?"

Major Starly nods in the affirmative.

Sun retrieves the sword cane. "I will keep this as a souvenir of our meeting. Good night, Major."

Sue Chen has been standing by to act as interpreter, if needed. "Christian, take my message and put it in correct English." Sun stares at the mountaintops as he composes his thoughts. "Address it to Commander James Stanhope-Owston, British Military *Attaché,* in care of Red Cross Mission, Shanghai. Major John Starly is my prisoner. I do not recognize your white flag. My ransom demand for his safe release is one million British pounds sterling. For the Americans, Van Halsted and his wife, I demand 200,000 United States dollars in gold certificates. For each of the four American college girls, I demand 50,000 United States dollars in gold certificates. Should you attempt to rescue my hostages, I will shoot the two adults and toss the four young women to my men for their pleasure. You have ten days to meet my demands. Lastly, I demand immunity for my men and myself, and that we be incorporated into the Shantung militia. Sun Mei-yao. Chinese Bandit Extraordinaire. Patu-ku Mountains, Shantung Province."

"Read it carefully, and ensure that it is correct, else you will stand at the whipping post."

"Yes, of course. I understand." She reads her message several times and tweaks a few points to make it exactly correct. "Bandit Sun, it is correct."

"You are positive, Christian Sue Chen?"

"I would not be so stupid as to incur your anger and punishment. This message is correct, as you dictated."

"Very well. Put it in an envelope, and address it to that British commander."

"I have already accomplished that task." She shows Sun the addressed envelope.

Somewhat flustered that Chen correctly anticipated him, he demands, "Bring that Red Cross porter to me."

On arrival, Sun tells the fellow, "Sergeant Hsu Su-en will escort you to the base of the mountain. Return as you came, in those Japanese trucks. In Shanghai, you will hand this envelope to Commander Stanhope-Owston personally and to no one else. Understand?"

The porter is so intensely afraid that he cannot speak. He nods his head in affirmation.

"Chen, quiz this fellow to ensure that he knows and will comply."

Shortly, she says, "He is ready and will fulfill your instructions accurately and promptly." She pauses to gather mental strength. "May I suggest that you give him a dozen Mexican silver pesos to motivate him, and promise him a dozen more on completion of his task?"

Sun fumes inside. Again, Chen has bested him in strategy. *By my ancestors, that she-devil Christian is clever. Perhaps, I should take her as my wife.* "Excellent suggestion, Sue Chen, do so."

13

British Legation, International Settlement, Shanghai.
0900 hours, 15–17 May, 1923

"**D**amn that bloody bastard! Sun has taken Starly hostage and demands one million pounds ransom," fumes Commander James Stanhope-Owston. "It's unconscionable that he would violate the civilized convention of the white flag." He crumples Sun's message and tosses it across the room. "That debased scoundrel has just signed his death warrant."

Cholmondeley Alastair retrieves the ruffled message, reads it, and comments, "That rips the equation." He grimaces. Alastair is well aware that Captain Sir Mansfield George Smith-Cumming, KCMB, CG, Head of the Secret Intelligence Service at Broadway House, will be outraged; he has a propensity for "killing" messengers who bring untoward news. Alastair rereads the message and says, with a touch of humor in his voice, "Clearly, this bandit Sun fellow was not raised on the playing fields of Eton."

Alastair takes an MI6 message form and carefully details the current intelligence *re* Sun's treachery. He pushes the intercom and buzzes for a cipher clerk.

Almost immediately, a young woman with a daring mien enters. In a mocking voice, she speaks as if she were in service, "You rang, *sir-r-r?*"

Alastair cracks a thin smile at her inside *bon mot,* and moving images unreel in his mind of her *au naturale,* lying in his bed. "Mistress Prudence, send this FLASH message to London, and include the War Office and the *chargé d'affaires* in Peiping. Use the KZ code."

"Very well, sir." Seeing that her attempt at flirtation has flopped, she makes a *faux* adjustment to her too short and too tight flapper skirt and says, "I will have it zinging through the ether within fifteen minutes." She shakes her head, causing her flaming red hair to cascade over her left shoulder. "Anything else, sir?"

"Not now, Mistress Prudence. Not now." He winks.

Alastair knows full well that London will not take Sun's chicanery lightly. Bandits do not twist the lion's tail without consequences. *Surely the War Office will order a mini-scale military campaign. I will need to have all the intelligence I can muster.* "Commander, quiz that porter fellow and find out what he saw at Sun's hideaway."

"Right. My Mandarin is a touch rusty, but here goes." Stanhope-Owston points to the Chinese porter and motions for him to come closer. The fellow carefully approaches, fearful that the commander will exercise his anger on him. He motions for the porter to sit, and hands him a ten pound note. "That's for your trouble and for your cooperation. We want to know all that you saw and heard at the bandit's hideaway. Understand?"

The porter's eyes are wide as he stares at the British currency—more money than he'd earn in a year. He stuffs the bill in his pocket and nods his head up and down several times. "Yes, sir. I understand, sir."

Stanhope-Owston gets what information he can. Unfortunately, the porter did not make note of the things he saw. However, he does recall key details about Sun's compound, his military preparations, and a few redoubts on the down slope. Lastly, he tells of Starly's failed attempt to impale Sun with his rapier.

Stanhope-Owston shouts, "Damn!"

"What the news?"

Stanhope-Owston comments with intensity, "That Major Starly still has his *esprit de corps*. Starly tried to impale Sun with his sword cane. That's British pluck."

"I would not have guessed that Starly had such aggression in him. Reckon Passchendaele never dies."

During the hubbub, the porter slips out of the room.

Alastair buzzes the intercom. "Send in a stenographer." Shortly, a tall, middle-aged woman with bobbed hair enters and stands by his desk. He asks Stanhope-Owston, "Please dictate that fellow's comments to Gwendolyn. She'll edit his babblings into a formal report and type it in triplicate."

Gwendolyn says in a falsetto voice, "Is that all, *sir-r-r?*" She cracks a small, knowing smile.

Alastair misses the taunt. He frowns deeply, his eyes narrow, and he asks of anyone within hearing, "Did we get that fellow's signature on an Official Secrets Act document?"

他處.

Ten Downing Street, London.
1000 hours, 15 May 1923

Prime Minister Sir Stanley Baldwin, in controlled anger, demands of Edward George Stanley, First Secretary of the War Office, "Prepare a military expedition to rescue the hostages and raise a terrible vengeance on that duplicitous Chinese bandit Sun Mei-yao." Baldwin rereads Alastair's MI6 message. "Sun demands ransom payment in nine days, else he'll murder his hostages." He adjusts his glasses. "Mister Stanley, is that bandit serious or bluffing?"

Edward Stanley contributes, "Minister Baldwin, we cannot take a chance that Sun is bluffing. However, I would suggest that murdering the hostages would be inimical to his advantage—foolish, it would be. He would lose his leverage for ransom, and he knows, no matter what, we'll come after him to extract our pound of flesh, as it were."

He adds, "Prime Minister, please understand we have no regular army detachment stationed in China. We'll muster a military command in Shanghai and forge an international brigade from our disparate commands and the Occidentals' military. By necessity, it will be a pell-mell of units from several nations with unknown fighting ability. Nonetheless, the officers will do their best to hone the brigade to a proficient fighting force." He looks at his notes. "I'll send my orders immediately."

Baldwin responds, "Do it. Pay no ransom. Rescue the hostages by whatever ploy, and do what's necessary. Inform me when you have the hostages, and so forth."

他處.

Military Headquarters, Fort Canning, Singapore.
1000 hours, 16 May 1923

A cipher clerk enters the office of Lieutenant General Sir Heathcliff Percival-Trengove, GC, DSO. "Sir, I have a For Your Eyes Only message for you. It's classified Most Secret, Special Access, Code Word Lambda."

The general grabs the message, scans it, and then rereads it carefully. A wide grin crawls over his face. A few seconds later, the general barks at the message clerk, "Dismissed." He reflects for several minutes, lights up a cigar, and with a spring in his step walks out of his office. "Brigadier! It's here. I have my orders to Shanghai. I am to form a command to rescue those hostages from the damn bandit, Sun." He slaps the paper with the back of his hand.

Executive Officer, Brigadier General, Sir Edward Arthur Fanshaw, KCB, grins ear to ear. "Congratulations, Heathcliff. It's time that we run those yellow blighters to ground."

Lieutenant General Sir Percival-Trengove chomps on his cigar. "I'm leaving Singapore this afternoon on that Gosport Flying Boat at Port Stanley. As of now, Brigadier, you are the commanding officer of all His Majesty's forces in Singapore, Malaya Straits, Sarawak, North Borneo, and Brunei. Paperwork to follow."

The brigadier snaps to attention and, with a formal salute, says, "Yes, sir. Godspeed and good hunting."

他處.

British Military Command Center, International Settlement, Shanghai.
0900 hours, 17 May1923

"Damn! Where are those British Marines?" shouts Lieutenant General Percival-Trengove. "Find them, Commander Stanhope-Owston, and get them integrated into our brigade—such as it is. They're to lead the attack." He surveys the hubbub from his makeshift command center. He understands all too clearly that petty jealousies, and entrenched prerogatives of British inter-service commands, foreign bureaucrats, and their military commanders have mired the formation of his multi-service and multinational brigade into a disparate assemblage, which would not be capable of competing in a cricket match. *Forming this expedition is a flapdoodle. We've only eight days to rescue those hostages—mostly American colonials, I understand. Damn this posting. My Singapore command is much more attractive, and the bandits be damned.*

  He recalls the FLASH, Most Secret wireless messages he sent to the Commander, British East-Asia Squadron, and the military *attaché* in Peiping, requesting troops and equipment for his rescue mission: infantry from the British legations in Peiping, Canton, and Shanghai; British Marines from ships in ports; and naval infantry from the gunboats on the Yangtze and Yellow Rivers: the *HMS Dragonfly, Grasshopper, Locust,* and *Mosquito.* From the second floor of the Command Center, he looks out his bay window onto the parade ground and sees chaos—the men are milling about smartly. *Not a combat-trained man in the bunch.* The deputy he designated as Commanding Officer of the brigade is ineffective. *Too much office work and not enough fighting experience,* he muses. Parochialism prevails. The men reluctantly obey commands from officers they do not know and they natter aimlessly. *There's no chance that we can mold that motley crew into a competent fighting force within the next few days. Our casualties will be excessively high, Sun will massacre his hostages, and the bandits will escape justice. Damn!*

  His deep frown fades as a sly grin creeps over his face. *Perhaps not all is lost.* He watches the Gurkha platoon from Nanking perform combat drills, load cartridges into magazines, clean their weapons, and sharpen their kukri blades. *Those Nepalese blighters are going to be hard to control—they'll be bent on seeking revenge for the massacre of their brothers at Lincheng.*

The General reviews the military contingents from the other Occidental embassies whose citizens were murdered: two squads of naval infantry from the French destroyer *Cassiopeia,* and a detachment of twenty Italian soldiers from their Treaty Port of Amoy. *A sorry lot, indeed.* He opens his desk drawer, withdraws a bottle of Scotch whiskey, pours a healthy drink, and swigs it down. At the window again, he spots a company of the White Russian Volunteer Corps performing synchronized physical fitness drills. *Who ordered the Russians? At least they're not Red Bolsheviks. No Americans yet. What colonial bumpkins will their military attaché send?*

The whiskey deepens his black mood. At the sound of a snappy, "Good morning, General," he looks up and sees a 'spit and polish' United States Marine in his dress blues, standing stiffly at attention with his right hand in a formal salute. On his left chest is an impressive array of medals; draped across his chest is the bright silk sash of the *Ordre national de la Légion d'honneur,* and draped about his neck are the Medal of Honor ribbon and insignia.

Stunned at first by this tall and fit American Marine with an exemplary military mien, and then impressed by his obviously sterling combat record and heroism, Lieutenant General Percival-Trengove stands, returns the salute, and says, "Report."

"Sir, Master Sergeant Shaun McKenna, United States Marine Corps with two squads of marines from the United States battle cruiser *USS Huron,* flagship of the East Asia Squadron, reporting for duty." He hands the general the orders for his detail. Without a flinch, he asks impatiently, "Where are those bandits, sir? We'll bring back the hostages." He checks his watch. "We can shove off in thirty minutes. We have transport, and are well armed—awaiting your command."

A small smile of admiration creeps across Lieutenant General Percival-Trengove's face and his despondency fades rapidly. The American standing before him is just the sort of soldier he needs to whip his brigade into a proficient military organization. "Welcome to my command, Master

Sergeant McKenna. I admire your *espirt de corps*—exactly what this outfit needs. However, understand that you and your men will be integrated into an international brigade and, working in concert, we'll rescue the hostages and bring that bandit Sun and his gang to British justice."

He still stands at attention, but a frown creeps across the sergeant's face. He responds sharply, "Aye, aye, sir. On your orders."

"Sit down, Master Sergeant. I've never had an American in my command." Unabashedly, the general stares at the sergeant's multiple decorations. "Tell me about your background. Have a cup of coffee. Better yet, let's have a Scotch whiskey, straight."

Not used to dealing with generals, Sergeant McKenna eases into the chair in front of the general's desk. "Thank you, sir. Coffee is welcome. However, with all due respect, it is not my place to socialize with a general officer."

Lieutenant General Percival-Trengove, slightly miffed at the master sergeant's rebuff, recovers quickly. "Yes, indeed, Master Sergeant. My error. I see that you've been soldiering for some time. Tell me about your campaigns."

His face flushed red with embarrassment, Sergeant McKenna responds, "As you request, General." Without looking at his decorations, he responds, "Manila Bay, 1898; International Settlement Peiping, 1900; Baliuay and Quingua, Philippine Islands; Nicaragua, 1912; Veracruz, 1914; Dominican Republic, 1914; Sonora, Mexico, the Pancho Villa chase, 1916; Belleau Wood and Chateâu-Tiery, France, 1918; Vladivostok, 1920; bandit suppression near Foochow, 1921; and other minor campaigns."

"My God! Master Sergeant McKenna, that's a record *sans pareil.* What's the background on your Purple Heart medal with the four oak-leaf clusters?"

"Nothing serious, sir."

Realizing that the sergeant prefers not to relate the circumstances of his combat wounds, the general says, "I understand, Master Sergeant."

His batman brings coffee in a silver service with obviously expensive Wedgwood china He places a saucer and cup in front of the general and the sergeant. Knowing the general's preferences, he adds a lump of sugar and a small dash of cream. "Master Sergeant?"

Uncomfortable with the formal folderol, McKenna stares at the china in front of him. "Black," he blurts. A second later, he adds in a softer voice, "Please."

"Master Sergeant McKenna, you are the man I need to get this so-called brigade in fighting trim. The politics and petty jealousies have overcome military discipline. Most of the men have no combat experience and little interest in our mission."

Percival-Trengove looks at Master Sergeant McKenna for a few seconds. He takes a long drink from his coffee, and then puts the cup down a touch too hard. "It has been years since I've commanded a fighting outfit. I've become a paper pusher and a paperclip counter." He lowers his voice and his faces flushes bright red. "I've not recovered my command authority, I'm embarrassed to confide."

Master Sergeant McKenna turns away from the general and stares out a window. He drains his cup and his mind whirls as he recalls a number of times in combat when his superior officers were ineffective, leaving him to take command. "I understand, sir."

Still flushed red, the general continues, "Excellent, Master Sergeant." He beams, as he now has the *deus ex machina* to save his command. "Effective immediately, you are the Sergeant Major of this command, and you report directly to me."

Sergeant Major McKenna stands and straightens an imaginary crease in his trousers. "Aye, aye, sir."

Understanding proper military protocol, Lieutenant General Percival-Trengove stands at attention and salutes Master Sergeant McKenna. "It is I that render honors to you, Master Sergeant McKenna with your Medal of Honor."

McKenna returns the general's salute. "On your orders, General."

"At ease, Master Sergeant. We've only eight days to shape this brigade into an efficient fighting force and to rescue the hostages. If anyone, officer or not, gives you grief, tell them to complain to me. I'll pass a general order to the troops immediately, confirming your appointment and authority."

"Aye, aye, sir."

14

Bandit Sun's Hideaway, Patu-ku Mountains, Shantung Province. 1400 hours, 17 May 1923

The super heterodyne sings with the harmonious tune of short and long bursts of the electrical energy of radiotelegraphy. Ch'uan Feng artfully transcribes the incoming message's dots and dashes into information. On completion, he runs to Sun Mei-yao, who is working with Sergeant Tang Tse-che and his machine gun crews. The multiple *rat-tat-tat-tats* are deafening. The fellow tugs at Sun's sleeve to get his attention. He shouts, "Our friend in Shanghai has sent us an urgent message. Just decoded."

Sun whirls around, grabs the message from the operator, and reads it. "You are positive this is decoded correctly?"

"Yes, sir. I have double-checked the text and it is true."

"Very well. Get back to your radio. Acknowledge receipt, and tell our friend to keep me apprised of changes promptly."

Sun's eyes narrow and a deep frown creases his forehead. He shouts to no one, "A wrathful curse on those duplicitous Englanders!" *They are going to attack me with an international coalition of Occidental troops. I don't understand. They have disregarded my threat to kill the hostages. I want no fight. I want the ransom money and immunity.* He retreats to his office in the Headquarters Building to gather his thoughts and to form a strategy.

He reads the message again, this time with extreme care. He notes that the Occidental brigade will have about three hundred and fifty men—a collage of British and other European troops, mostly non-combat. He opens the bottom desk drawer and withdraws a bottle of rare Macallan Scotch whiskey that he purloined from the Shanghai Express. He drinks directly from the bottle. The intoxicating beverage warms his soul. He reflects. *They have no artillery, a couple of old mortars, and only a few machine guns.* His disposition improves. With false bravado, he exclaims to his portrait tacked on the wall, "With my strong defensive positions, trained men, and modern weapons, we will destroy that Occidental brigade in short order."

Disturbing his self-assurance is a nagging thought festering in the back of his brain that he cannot bring to the fore. He swigs again and again. Shortly, "the Americans" races into clear focus. *The Americans!* He sits upright. *What of the Americans? No mention of their contingent in this message.* He swigs deeply and a devilish grin creeps across his face as he recalls the particulars of a course taught on insurgency at the Whampoa Military Academy. *These Americans are tomfools and of no import. It took them three bloody years to defeat the guerrilla Emilio Aguinaldo in the Philippines. Bandit Pancho Villa evaded them for a year in the Sonoran Desert, and the Americans retreated in defeat across the border into Texas. Their interventions in the banana wars in Central America were a disaster.* He stares at the identification photographs of the American college girls pasted on the opposite wall. *I wonder.*

Sun drinks deeply of the intoxicating liquid. A few moments later, he tilts his chair back, and with a touch of *élan* places his boots on the desk. His mind whirls with possible strategies to parry the Occidentals' threat—none seem viable. He sees phantoms dancing in front of him—each dangles the hangman's noose. He shouts loudly to his messenger. "Get Captain Chao Tan-keng!"

The fellow rushes into the office. He is well-acquainted with Sun's wrath at incompetent performance. "Very well, Bandit Sun. I go."

A few minutes later, a soft voice from the doorway rouses Sun from his pensive musings. "May I be of service?" His most exotic concubine smiles coquettishly. "All options available."

A slow smile crosses Sun's face as he peruses the cheongsam-clad, startlingly beautiful female. He quickly runs down her list of 'options.' "You tempt me mightily, woman." He sits upright, looks away, and says, "Later, perhaps."

She strikes a titillating pose to ensure that the thigh-high split in her cheongsam displays her long and shapely leg to its most entrancing advantage. "I shall prepare for later."

"As you will." He shuffles papers on his desk. "For now, I must cleanse my mind of your 'options,' imaginary phantoms, and Scotch whiskey vapors." Sun flicks the back of his right hand toward the concubine—his signal for her to leave. "Bring tea."

Executive Officer Chao Tan-keng knocks on Sun's door and enters. He forgoes the formalities of standing at attention and giving a snappy salute. He's out of breath and is soaked in perspiration. "Sorry for the delay, Sun, I was working with the Second Battalion on bayonet practice." Without asking permission, he plops into the chair next to Sun's desk. "Our soldiers are getting more proficient every day. In a week, they will be first-class professionals in close quarters combat."

"Commendable, Chao." Without ado, Sun says with concern, "Our scheme for a peaceful ransom for our hostages is not going as straightforwardly as we had planned." He picks up the message and waves it back and forth a few times. "Evil spirits haunt our compound. Earlier this morning, I received this communication from our agent. The Englanders are forming an Occidental brigade to rescue the hostages and, I suspect, to either hang or imprison us. I have no doubt the former is their first option." He scans the message again. "The missing intelligence is the composition and competence of the American contingent." He forces a crooked smile. "From their past wartime performance, I would suspect that we do not have much concern with these bumpkins."

In a troubled voice, Chao responds, "Bandit Sun, do not dismiss the Americans so cavalierly. In 1918, during the Great War, they were instrumental in routing the Germans on the Western Front." After a brief pause, he asks, "And the rest of the brigade?"

"Our friend reports that it is a motley crew of mostly non-combat troops—service corps types, legation guards, naval infantry, and various military garrison personnel." Sun reflects for a few seconds. "My initial conclusion was that we would defeat the Westerners easily." The concubine returns with a magnificent Ming blue tea service. She glances at Chao and smiles in acknowledgement. She pours the piping hot oolong tea with exquisite grace. On Sun's signal, she leaves, her *derrière* swinging erotically.

Sun is oblivious to the concubine's flirtation. He sips the tea, looks at Chao, and in an agitated voice demands, "We have two options: fight or flee. What say you, Chao?"

After slight reflection, Chao answers in a strong voice, "Let's fight. Our troops are well trained and most have combat experience; our armory is stocked with an abundant supply of excellent weapons and ammunition. Our machine-gun crews are demonstrably proficient. Hidden in the redoubts on the down slope, their enfilade fire will annihilate the Occidentals approaching from the plain. Snipers will keep them pinned down. Should any of them survive to the pass, we'll greet them with rifle fire and bayonets. Chinese mettle will prevail."

Sporting a sly grin, Sun rubs his cheeks and speaks with authority. "An excellent scenario, Chao. We would defeat their assault the first time. And the second time. And even the third. Sooner or later, however, they will have reinforcements, heavy artillery, and air power. The Occidentals will overcome us. And you and I will be in the hangman's noose."

Chao hears Sun's words. He slumps in his chair and cradles his head with both hands. He makes coarse, inaudible sounds. *We are plagued with demons.* He sits upright, and in a soft voice says, "You speak truthfully, Sun. In the long term, we will lose." He sips tea to ease his disappointment.

The tea's steaming vapors have subsided. Sun brushes the teacup aside. "If we flee, we must have a long lead and a secure hideaway far from any British- or Occidental-controlled areas. Perhaps in Japan or Chosen." He reaches for the lukewarm tea, then decides against it. "We will be safe for a while. Nonetheless, the British will not forget our assault on their train and our killing their subjects. INTERPOL will have our pictures on wanted posters in every police station in the civilized world, and offer a handsome reward for our capture, dead or alive." He rises and looks out a window at his troops honing their fighting skills.

Chao, confronted with the sober realities of either plan, reviews their options. "If we flee, we must release the hostages, probably to Priester Lenfers, and escape with what booty we can." He stares at Sun. "We will abandon our men to their fate, which is a risky option. Those not killed or captured in the assaults will have a passionate desire for revenge against us for our betrayal."

Returning to his chair, Sun responds, "Point made, Chao."

"Bandit Sun, do we fight? If not, we are kowtowing to the white man as our ancestors did for hundreds of years with their unequal treaties, extra-territorial jurisdiction in our cities, disdain of our ancient religion, British opium, and other indignities to our culture." He stands and demands, "Sun, do we fight or flee?"

Sun does not respond. He stares out the window and sees his burgeoning army training for the upcoming conflict.

He turns to Chao and, in a forceful voice, answers, "We fight! We do not kowtow to the Occidentals."

Chao says with soaring confidence, "No matter how many assaults, we will persevere!"

"Not true, Chao. We will fight vigorously during the first assault and inflict heavy casualties on the Occidentals." He sips the tea. It's cool. In a flash of anger, he brushes the Ming blue cup and saucer onto the floor and they shatter. "After the first attack, they will need several days to regroup and prepare for another offensive. During this lull, we'll flee. Prepare!"

15

Aerodrome, International Settlement, Shanghai.
0500 hours, 18 May 1923

"Switch off!"

"Switch off."

"Clear!"

"Clear."

The mechanic turns the propeller through four rounds. He shouts, "Contact!"

"Contact," responds the cockpit.

The mechanic snaps one blade downward and steps aside smartly.

The Rolls-Royce Falcon's V12 engine roars to life with a thunderous cacophony. The World War I Bristol Fighter F2b, a two-seater, begins to roll as the aviator advances the throttle. The F2b gains speed, becomes airborne, and turns toward Shantung Province on an aerial reconnaissance mission.

The aviator is Mister Trevor Lyndon, former Lieutenant in the Royal Naval Air Service, credited with sinking one U-boat in the Great War. Lyndon is the aerodrome manager. In the back seat is Mister Miles Prichard, former color-sergeant photographer wounded by a Turkish bullet in the Mesopotamian Campaign. He is armed with his newly purchased Leica model "O" 35mm camera. Prichard is staff photographer for *The Shanghai Times*.

Commander James Stanhope-Owston devised this covert aerial reconnaissance mission, commandeered the Bristol fighter, and inveigled the crew from the British Aero Club for this special twelve-hour, two-fueling-stops flight over Sun's hideout. Apprised of the importance and dangers in the mission, Lyndon and Prichard readily agreed to participate. Stanhope-Owston understood that their patriotic service to King and Country demonstrated in the Great War remained unswerving.

他處.

Sun's Hideaway, Patu-ku Mountains, Shantung Province.
0930 hours, 18 May 1923

Sun reviews the new message from his friend in Shanghai. "Here, Chao, what do you make of this?"

Chao reads the message an reflects for a few seconds. "This portends serious trouble. That en route reconnaissance aeroplane will overfly our compound in about an hour. Their camera will garner significant intelligence about our defensive positions and order of battle. Coupled with our friend's other messages, we must conclude that the Occidental brigade is near combat-ready." He reaches into his pocket for a cigarette, lights it with a match, and takes a deep drag. The smoke drifts lazily upward. "With the intelligence the English derive from the aerial photography, their assault will be much more aggressive and effective than we had planned."

"Exactly." Sun desperately wants a stiff gulp of that Scotch in his desk drawer at headquarters. "That accursed British intelligence is as devious as their vile reputation. Aerial reconnaissance!" He looks at the cloudless blue sky and curses. Then he notices that his flag hangs limp in the still air. He offers a silent prayer to his ancestors for rain and high winds—anything to thwart that Bristol aircraft's mission. "Captain Chao, to my office. Let us reflect on our strategy."

"Share this excellent Scotch with me." The pair sits silently and sips the dark liquid. After a time, Chao offers, "I will position several machine guns as anti-aircraft weapons and order the men to fire their rifles at the Bristol fighter."

"Very well," Sun responds with minimal enthusiasm. Two swigs later, and now slightly inebriated, Sun opines, "Chao, we are close to having a losing hand. The Occidentals are more determined and resourceful than I would have imagined." He shuffles some papers and scans an earlier message. He looks out the window at his First Battalion practicing hand-to-hand combat. His eyes narrow. "No matter how many battles we win, we loose the war." He withdraws a silver case from his blouse and lights a cigarette. "How goes your preparations for our escape? Sub rosa, of course?"

"Progressing to a completion within a few days."

Sun again reads another of the recent messages from his friend. He fidgets in his chair and swigs again. "I underestimated those Americans. I never would have figured that one of their sergeants could form that mob of would-be soldiers into a fighting force. I must meet this Sergeant Major Shaun McKenna of the United States of America Marine Corps."

Chao says, "We shall. And soon."

"Yes, indeed we shall. I will post a bounty on his head of 10,000 dollars—Chinese, of course."

Chao counters, "Meanwhile, I will send scouts into the province and get our machine guns in the redoubts."

With a concerned voice Sun orders, "Do it. Now."

池 l 多

At 1400 hours, Sergeant Hsu Su-en hears the faint hum of the Bristol fighter's Rolls-Royce Falcon engine. He dashes to the large gong near the tea house and pounds it ten times with the mallet, sounding the alarm. The thunderous sound reverberates heavily throughout the hideout. The well-drilled soldiers bolt for their defensive positions. Machine gunners snap bolts back and let the first rounds slam home in the breeches. Soon, every man hears the roar of the aircraft's engine. Sun, with a deep frown, stands by the tea house and has his rifle at the ready. *We cannot let this British aeroplane escape with that camera.*

Trevor Lyndon, expecting intense incoming fire, jams the throttle forward and the Bristol accelerates to its top speed of 120 miles per hour.

He adjusts the altitude to about 1,200 feet above the valley floor. He glances at Miles Prichard in the rear cockpit and gives a thumbs up.

Prichard responds with his own thumbs up. On his Leica is a medium telephoto lens, and the camera's appropriate f-stop and highest shutter speed are set.

Lyndon guides the Bristol to the plains on the western side of Sun's mountain compound and aligns the aeroplane on a west-east flight line.

Prichard instantly recalls his aerial combat missions in the Near East, leans over the cockpit, and views the rapidly passing scene of the plains through his viewfinder. As the Bristol starts its run over Sun's compound, he triggers the shutter time and time again, taking low oblique photographs. Incoming tracers lace the sky. Regular rounds are deadly phantoms unseen. Generally, the rounds fly behind the Bristol because Sun's men have not been trained to lead a fast-moving target. Near the end of the run, Prichard screams and drops his Leica. A bullet has slammed into his right leg. Fortunately, the neck strap keeps the camera from falling. He grimaces in pain. *Damn! It's the desert campaign over again.* Blood pumps out his wound—an artery is seriously nicked.

The Bristol completes its first pass. Lyndon notices a few holes in the wing fabric and one seriously close to the petrol tank. He pilots the Bristol clear of the compound, eases back the throttle, and banks right for another run. *A second run over a target is pure insanity. The gunners are learning how to lead.* He checks with Prichard.

Prichard forces a grin and gives a thumbs up.

Lyndon guides the Bristol aeroplane over an adjacent and parallel east-west flight line and advances the throttle. The ground fire is intense and more accurate. Holes pop throughout the Bristol—several stringer wires are cut. Fortunately, no key components are hit.

Prichard, struggling in pain, commands all his mental and physical resources to continue his oblique photography. As the Bristol completes the last run, he slumps back in his seat and clasps the Leica tightly to his chest.

Sun is livid. "You idiots!" he shouts. "Curses on you and your ancestors. Everyone's pay is cut twenty-five percent. You cannot hit a target as big as that aeroplane—as low as it was flying—and bring it to ground? Incompetence reigns in this compound. Your bumbling will effect your death in a few days. The Occidentals now have detailed intelligence about us."

A deathly silence suffuses throughout the hideaway. Then, a scattering of low-volume nattering pervades it. Sun stomps to headquarters and his Scotch bottle.

池阝号

Aerodrome, Nan Chang, Kiangsu Province.
1930 hours, 18 May 1923

Two hours later, Trevor Lyndon aligns the Bristol for landing on the dirt airstrip at Nan Chang in Kiangsu Province. The adrenaline rush he had over the target has left him tired and a little shaky. Touchdown is smooth and the roll out even. He taxies to a shack that has a large Socony Vacuum Service sign painted in English and in Chinese ideographs. When the Bristol comes to a stop, two attendants run to it and chock the wheels. Lyndon points to the petrol tank in the upper wing. Immediately, the fellows establish a bucket brigade to bring petrol to the Bristol.

Lyndon climbs out of the cockpit, slips to the ground, stomps his feet to increase circulation, and wipes the oil off his goggles and face. He shouts, "Hey, Miles, that was a bloody blast, not so? Got good photographs?"

Miles Prichard does not respond.

Lyndon climbs onto the lower wing and, for the first time, sees blood seeping out on it. He looks into Prichard's cockpit and sees him slumped in his seat; his dead eyes stare into space. "My God!" *I had no idea Miles was hit.* He spots the Leica clasped to Prichard's breast. With tender care, he removes the bloodied camera and sees that the film counter is at zero. *He's exposed all the frames.*

"'Best of British' Colour-Sergeant Miles Pritchard," Lyndon whispers; he salutes a fellow 'Tommy,' and makes the sign of the cross.

池阝昌

After making arrangements with the local constabulary to have Prichard's remains sent to Shanghai on the next train, Lyndon guns the Bristol and sets a course for Shanghai. The Leica is strapped around his neck.

16

MI6 Spaces, British Legation, International Settlement, Shanghai.
0400 hours, 19 May 1923

$\mathcal{P}$etty Officer Brian Crutchfield peers through a stereoscopic viewer at the eight inch by ten inch photographs. With the sure eyes of an experienced photographic interpreter, he circles targets of interest with a red crayon-pencil. He deftly annotates the next photograph. It takes him only two hours to complete the analysis of all thirty-six photographs taken by Miles Prichard.

Commander James Stanhope-Owston then marks and annotates the targets on his small-scale map of the Patu-ku Mountains. At midmorning, Stanhope-Owston and Crutchfield complete a detailed Essential Elements of Information intelligence report. They have plotted a comprehensive layout of Sun's compound and spotlighted placement of his key defensive positions, troop deployments, and machine gun redoubts. Of singular import, Crutchfield has discovered Sun's secret backdoor entrance.

Commander Stanhope-Owston hands the EEI package to Petty Officer Rolfe Ferguson, station photographer. "Make ten copies. I need them no later than 1300."

"Will do, sir."

池口壽

British Legation, International Settlement, Shanghai.
1030 hours, 19 May 1923

An eight-foot concrete wall, inset with metal spikes, surrounds the British Legation compound. The grounds are meticulous: trim shrubbery, rose gardens, a maze of in-season flowerbeds, and a large bed of poppies with a single white cross inscribed:

> *In Flanders fields the poppies blow*
> *Between the crosses, row on row*

Atop the headquarters building is an array of specialized radio antennae.

A walk-in vault is in a back room of the radio-message center. Access is denied to all except two Royal Navy enlisted petty officers. They hold the Most Secret, Special Intelligence Omega security clearance. The vault houses an array of specialized electronic equipment, one of which is the newly arrived machine from the Computing-Tabulating-Recording Company.

Chief Petty Officer Telegraphist James Cotterile is in mufti, his regular attire. He checks that he has stamped the three messages with the correct security classification. He slips the messages and the *communiqués* from MI6 London into a manila folder, seals it with stout tape, places the folder into a thick leather valise, and spins the vault's combination lock closed. He withdraws his Webley 455 revolver from the holster on his hip, flicks open the cylinder, and sees that it is fully loaded.

A few minutes later, Cotterile says, "Mister Alastair, I have urgent information."

"Very well, let's see."

Alastair scans the three messages. "Gawd blimey!" His eyes flash wide in stupefied surprise. A deep frown creases his forehead and he uses his left hand to rub his forehead and chin. "This can't be." He rereads them—this time with singular care. He snaps, "Cotterile, confirm."

"I've tripled-checked. These messages were sent in a simple code that our new decoding machine broke in six minutes. As to authenticity, the hand on the telegraph key has a distinctly unorthodox rhythm. I'd recognize it anywhere."

"What else?"

Cotterile withdraws the MI6 *communiqués* and hands them to Alastair. They are marked "Most Secret, Special Intelligence Omega, Eyes Only, Cholmondeley Alastair." Alarms ring in his brain. The heading is from the Chief of the Secret Intelligence Service, Captain, Sir Mansfield George Smith-Cumming. He reads for the gist, then absorbs every word, and eases into his chair. "Chief Cotterile, who else is privy to this information?"

In his most professional voice, Cotterile responds, "Only you and I."

"That's something." He releases a sigh. "Burn these messages and scatter the ashes."

"Aye, aye, sir."

池 阝彐

Brigade Training Area, International Settlement, Shanghai.
1300 hours, 19 May 1923

"You'll never kill a Chinese bandit that way," shouts Sergeant Major McKenna. He grabs the Carcano rifle, with bayonet attached, from the Italian soldier. McKenna charges the straw dummy, rams the bayonet into it, and thrusts it upward. "It is the upward thrust that makes the kill." He reaffirms with his hands. "Got it?"

"*Si, Sergente.*"

"Do it."

The Italian soldier tackles his bayonet-kill task with intense vigor. He looks to McKenna for confirmation. "*È che soddisfazzione?*"

"Well done, 'Itie," McKenna compliments. "Listen up, Trento. Get your fantail in gear and instruct the rest of your gang in how to kill bandits. Do it until those dummies are destroyed, completely. Understand?"

"*Il mio onore, sergente maggiore.*"

Trento cracks a big smile. He's honored at the *sergente maggioere's* approval and the assignment of responsibility.

McKenna hears a long string of *rat-tat-tat-tat-tat-tat* from the firing range. Within seconds, he's with the French crew that is firing a Hotchkiss machine gun. "Stand fast! *Arrêt poilu!*" he shouts. The firing ceases.

The corporal stands and addresses McKenna, "*Quelle, sergeant-major?*"

"*Anglais, sii vous plaît, corporel.*"

"*Oui,* sir. I understand a little."

"Corporal Farve, that continuous firing will burn out your gun in no time. Fire in short bursts—five or six rounds per burst. A short pause to let the gun cool. Fire again. Here's how." He kneels behind the Hotchkiss machine gun and fires six short bursts. "*Comprendre?*"

"Yes. Indeed. *Merci.*"

"Keep practicing. Change gunners every few minutes. There will be hostile incoming." He slaps the corporal on the back and says, "Carry on. Make Marianne proud of your crew."

With swelling pride, Corporal Farve says, "*Soyez assuré le sergeant-major.*"

Each day, under Sergeant Major McKenna's tireless and sterling command leadership, the battalion melds more and more into a top-notch international fighting force. Discipline and morale soar as the men increasingly take pride in their accomplishments. McKenna has become something of a demigod—he will lead, they will follow.

沪陸

Lieutenant General Percival-Trengove looks out the window of his office. He scans the practice grounds, the firing range, and the other areas where the men are training. A thin smile creeps over his face. He's immensely pleased at how quickly and efficiently Sergeant Major McKenna has transformed that mob of men into a well-honed fighting brigade. He works tirelessly and with compassion. *I see how he earned that chest full of awards. If we complete this rescue mission successfully and with minimum casualties, I will recommend him for the Royal Red Cross.*

Commander James Stanhope-Owston interrupts the general's ruminations with a "Good afternoon, General." He is carrying a large packet of documents and photographs under his left arm.

"Those are the EEIs?"

"Yes, sir. Shall I brief you?"

"Sure. Give me just the highlights. Meanwhile, I'll call a meeting of key personnel for a detailed briefing. Let's get started."

池陸

MI6 Spaces, British Legation, International Settlement Shanghai. 1830 hours, 19 May 1923

The planning room is empty. The area is deserted save for Cholmondeley Alastair, who is slouched in his chair. His eyes are closed.

Prudence sashays in and, in a radiant voice, exclaims, "Up, you blighter. Let's celebrate. Sergeant Major McKenna is honing the brigade into a serious fighting force; the aerial reconnaissance mission was a resounding success; and General Percival what's-his-name is in the Officers' Club, pontificating about his adventures during the Boxer Rebellion."

Her soft voice and exotic perfume stir Alastair to full attention. Delighted that his paramour is here, he wonders at the oxymoron: her name. "Prudence" belies her sexual appetite and proclivities. "Darling, you're just the antidote for my doldrums." He rises, grabs her in a deep hug, and kisses her passionately. "What's on your mind?"

"You rake. You know perfectly well." She smiles seductively. "Where shall it be?"

He grabs her arm and walks toward the door. "My flat." With an exuberant smile and a quick step, he offers, "I've a rare bottle of champagne that I've saved for a special occasion, and I'll cook for you one of the finest meals you ever tasted—an endless remembrance."

Several hours later, they lie in bed locked in each other's arms. Prudence, spent, is asleep. Alastair eases out of her embrace, enters his closet, and selects the one perfect silk tie—his regimental colors. He ties a knot in the center and slips on a pair of gloves.

Prudence slowly awakens and softly mumbles, "Come here, lover."

"Yes, lovely." In one swift motion, he loops the knotted tie around her neck and with both hands draws the *garrotte* tight.

Prudence has difficulty breathing. Instinctively, she grabs the *garrotte* with both hands to ease the pressure.

Alastair draws it a little tighter.

She gurgles with slightly jumbled words, "What the hell are you doing? Stop it. I can't breathe."

"That's the point, my dear spy for bandit Sun Mei-yao. I'm murdering you, Prudence Woodhalm. Or should I say, Sergeant Prudence O'Connell from the Irish Republican Army." He draws the *garrotte* a little tighter.

She gags and desperately tries to pull the *garrotte* from her neck. Her fingernails rip deep into Alastair's gloves. Reflexively, he slightly eases his grip. She desperately tries to say "No" and "Stop." Her words are babble.

"We see that your bank account in Hong Kong has several large deposits—some in British pounds sterling, others in Russian rubles, some in Japanese yen, some in French francs, and others in American dollars. From whom came those payments, my lovely? And the *pièce de résistance* is the hoard of Mexican silver pesos in your deposit box—favorite payment of bandit Sun Mei-yao. Rest assured, dear Prudence, the Secret Intelligence Service now has your funds in safe custody—they'll not migrate to the Irish Republican Army for terrorist activities." He tightens.

Her hands fall away and her eyes plead for relief.

"My, my, you have been a naughty girl, dear Prudence. London knows all the secrets you've passed to our adversaries." He pulls the *garrotte* as tight as he can.

A few minutes later, he dresses Prudence, carries her body to his automobile, and drives to a deserted wharf several miles up the Yangtze. He wraps her body in heavy-duty automobile chains and locks them tight. He slips her body into the dark, slowly flowing river. He gives a mocking salute. "Farewell, my lovely."

17

Yellow Sea, Offshore of the Shantung Peninsula.
0500 hours, 23 May 1923

The periscope breaks surface and twirls in a full circle. Within seconds, the sea erupts in foam as the jet-black submarine surfaces. The hatch in the conning tower cracks open and the skipper and the watch crew man their battle stations to search for anything that could betray them. Concurrently, the Chief Boatswain Mate and his boat-away crew climb out of the forward hatch. Five Gurkha commandos follow with a packaged rubber raft. The sergeant pops the carbon dioxide capsules and the boat snaps open. The 'Boats' and his crew lower the raft into the calm sea, and the commandos scramble aboard and paddle to shore. The submarine disappears.

The Gurkhas wade ashore, gather their equipment, deflate and bury the boat, and move inland. About four hours later, they are within sight of Sun's back door into the mountains—a small, sinuous road just wide enough for wagons and trucks. It's exactly where the photographic interpreter plotted it. Four bandits are about, supposedly guards. Two are asleep in the shade of birch trees, and two are smoking and chatting. Their machine gun is unmanned behind a sandbagged position. Copses of birch trees that surround the area provide the commandos cover. Within seconds, the skirmish is over. The Gurkas wipe the blood from their kukri knives. They trot up the road. At the two-mile mark, they bury mines on the road and booby-trap the areas around the mines. The sergeant continues upward. He spots the high ground, as shown in the briefing, plants a device in a rock crevice, turns on its battery, and camouflages it with leaves and small branches.

Tasks accomplished, the Gurkhas return to man the machine gun and hold the area.

他處.

Parade Ground, British Legation, International Settlement, Shanghai. 0800 hours, 23 May 1923

The Drum Major strikes his mace downward and the bagpipe and drum band plays the tune "The British Grenadiers" in quick time. The stirring music engulfs the parade ground in an invigorating martial ambiance. Sergeant Major McKenna stands stiffly at attention with his sword tucked below his right shoulder. His dress blue uniform is festooned with his medals and ribbons. Behind him are the guidon-bearers, hoisting their countries' flags. Following them are the officers and men of the Occidental brigade arrayed in classic military parade formation, each member in his dress uniform.

Lieutenant General Percival-Trengove stands on the elevated reviewing stand. The governor-generals of the Occidental communities in Shanghai, senior naval officers from ships in port, military *attachés*, Commander James Stanhope-Owston, Cholmondeley Alastair, and a few select civilians remain seated. The mayor of Shanghai and his coterie, and the commanding officer of the Chinese 21st battalion sit in front of the reviewing stand.

General Yoshinori Shirakawa, Commander of Japanese Forces in Central China, accompanied by his aides, watches with binoculars from the nearby Japanese Legation. He comments to his intelligence officer, "Make detailed notes and have the photographer take pictures with his telephoto lens." He raises his binoculars and continues watching the brigade's activities. "I do not trust those Britishers. But in this façade of cooperation, we will defer interference."

"General, the photographer is working now. And I am recording the brigade's activities."

To his operations officer, he says, "Send a message to Captain Ishihara Kanji, Commanding Officer of our naval base at Tsingtao: 'Cooperate completely with the Occidental brigade.' I expect a detailed report and photographs."

"Yes, General."

Sergeant Major McKenna stands five hundred feet from the review stand and calls, "Forrr-warrrd marrrch!" His booming voice echoes throughout the area. The brigade steps forward in unison and marches in methodical synchronization. The music, the flags, the brilliant colors, and the marching soldiers comprise a military pageant that engenders thrills and confidence in the thousands of Occidental and Chinese spectators.

"Eyeees right!" McKenna shouts and snaps his sword to the "present sword" position in salute while turning his head toward the general. In unison, the brigade follows his head movement , and the the guideons dip their flags.

Lieutenant General Percival-Trengove returns the salute, and the brigade passes in review.

迎阝專

MI6 Headquarters, British Legation, International Settlement, Shanghai. 1030 hours, 23 May 1923

Gwendolyn states in a demanding voice, "Mister Alastair, it's eleven thirty and Prudence is not here. I called her flat and there is no answer." She fidgets with her dress and asks in a soft and embarrassed voice, "Do you know her whereabouts?"

Without looking up, he responds with disdain, "No." He continues to work on his report.

She remains standing by his desk.

He looks at Gwendolyn with a sheepishly guilty grin. "We had dinner in my flat last evening. She left around two thirty. No need for alarm. She's been late from time to time."

By 1500 hours, Prudence still has not arrived and no one has heard from her. Alastair sends one of his agents to her flat. Using Alastair's key, the fellow inspects Prudence's flat. He tells Alastair, "Her bed is not mussed. Her automobile is in the garage and its engine is cold. In fact, I found nothing amiss."

The cipher clerk is missing.

As of 0900 hours the next day, Prudence remains absent. Because of her Most Secret, Compartmented clearance, Alastair now appears deeply concerned that something serious might be amiss. He checks with his staff and her friends—none has information about her. As a last resort, he calls Chief Inspector Duncan MacLeod of the Shanghai International Police and asks him to investigate Prudence's absence. "Duncan, keep this low profile. No leaks. No publicity. And a minimum of your officers involved."

MacLeod responds, "I understand very well, laddie. I worked for your outfit during the Great War." He pauses slightly, "Is it a matter of *cherchez la femme?*"

"Unknown. Perhaps you'll discover."

"I'll be in touch."

At sunset, Alastair receives a call from MacLeod. "Nothing. She has vanished—whether on her own volition or foul play, we cannot tell. She has not left Shanghai on public transportation. Of course, someone could have driven her out of the city. That is something we are unable to trace. If it were foul play, her body has not surfaced. I suspect that she is indulging in a tryst somewhere and will return shortly. Unless we receive a concrete clue, or someone volunteers information, there's not much we can do."

Seemingly stunned by MacLeod's report, Alastair says, "Thanks. Please keep on this case. We must find her or else know why she is absent without permission."

"Will do, ol' chum. But I'm pessimistic."

Alastair drafts a Missing Person message to MI6 London. He hands it to Gwendolyn. "Send this Priority, Most Secret, Zeta."

She scans the messages, and says in a pensive voice, "Yes, sir."

"No nattering, understand?"

"Of course." She fidgets for a couple of seconds and says, "If I may be so bold, Mister Alastair, I'm proud that you're taking Prudence's absence so seriously."

His eyes narrow and he frowns deeply. "I'm responsible for my people. And, I'm required to look after them." He forces a small smile. "Besides, I care for her deeply."

"I know, sir."

地 阝号

Later in the day, Gwendolyn opens a folder and hands Alastair a Most Secret, Zeta message from the Chief of MI6. He reads it and shakes his head in disbelief. He looks at the woman. "You've read it?"

"I decoded it."

"And?"

"I'm confused. London tells us that Prudence has resigned and is working for the NKK shipping lines in Tokyo." She dabs her handkerchief at tears on her cheeks. "And we are to suspend inquiries immediately. That's insanity." She tries to control her tears, unsuccessfully.

"Gwendolyn, I agree. There is a peculiar ambiance regarding Prudence's disappearance. Something is afoot. This morning Chief Inspector MacLeod and one of my men went to Prudence's flat to search for clues. They found it empty—nothing remained of her possessions. It was scrubbed clean. Not a speck of dust, not an untoward spot on anything, not one fingerprint; and her automobile is gone." He shakes his head. "I do not understand it either." He taps his pencil on his desk several times. "I reckon London knows of more things in heaven and earth than we might dream of."

She begins to bawl. Shortly she recovers, and says, "I'm sorry, sir. I was deeply attached to her—her mother hen, as it were."

"I know." Alastair forces another thin smile. "Gwendolyn, you've been with us almost three years, and your work and dedication are outstanding. Henceforth, you are our senior cipher clerk."

他處.

Radio Room, Bandit Sun's Hideaway, Shantung Province.
1420 hours, 23 May 1923

"It's true, Bandit Sun," Ch'uan Feng cries. "The radio is full of static. No matter which band or frequency, all I hear is a high-frequency buzzing."

"Fool, get off that stool. I shall tune this radio to the correct frequency!" shouts Sun. He manipulates the tuning dials to the assigned long-wave frequency where he expects to receive the telegraphic message from his friend in Shanghai. He hears the static. It permeates the radio spectrum. He slams his fist on the desk. He shouts in frustrated anger, "This radio is cursed. It is possessed with devils." He draws his Mauser pistol and aims it at the radio. "I will kill those demons!"

Chao puts his arm *on the pistol and gently pushes it downward. In a firm voice he says, "No. Sun, we need that radio. It's a British trick on us. It is the MI6 who are the devils."*

Calmer now, Sun replies, "You are correct, as always." He holsters his Mauser. "Our friend's message was due at 1400. I must have it. It is critical. It has updated information on the readiness status of the Occidental brigade, its battle plan, its departure date, and mode of transport." He states with finality, "We are blind without this intelligence."

他處.

Radio Room, British Legation, International Settlement, Shanghai.
1430 hours, 23 May 1923

The headphones on Commander James Stanhope-Owston emit a very low, eerie, high-frequency noise. "More volume, Chief."

Chief Petty Officer James Cotterile replies, "That's it, Commander. My jammer is low power. We are fortunate to receive that signal with our specialized equipment."

Stanhope-Owston slips off the phones and smiles broadly. "Well done, Chief."

Cotterile returns the smile and says, "It was fun. That bandit Sun can't receive or transmit a signal on any band. Kudos to the special operations Gurkha team that secreted my jamming device. I reckon its battery will function for three or four days."

涉阝導

Lieutenant General Percival-Trengove's Office, International Settlement, Shanghai. 1530 hours, 23 May 1923

Chief Petty Officer Telegraphist James Cotterile stands silently at attention in the foyer of Lieutenant General Percival-Trengove's office. Today he wears his Royal Navy dress blues. The general is talking with some of his officers about transport for the brigade. He spots Cotterile with a valise under his right arm. "Come in, Chief."

Cotterile does not move and says, "With respect, General."

Immediately the general understands. "Gentlemen, excuse me," he tells the men in the room. "We have covered the scheme and have worked out the details. Dismissed."

The rattling of papers, sounds of briefcases closing, and shuffling of feet signal the conclusion of the meeting.

The general says, "Last man out, close the door and stand guard outside—no one, and I mean no one, is to disturb me." After the door is closed, he says, "Let's have it."

Cotterile hands him the IMMEDIATE PRIORITY, Most Secret, Zeta message.

The general's eyes open wide. "No doubt that you've decoded this message with absolute surety and it is from the headline sender?"

"I've double-checked through the back channel and have confirmed that it is authentic."

"Thanks, Chief Petty Officer. Well done."

Cotterile says, "Thank you, General." He waits uneasily.

"Burn it."

"By your leave, General." He exits.

In the quiet of his office, Percival-Trengove pours brandy into a snifter and rotates it between his hands. He smells the aroma and sips the dark amber liquid several times. The message is from Sir Stanley Baldwin, Prime Minister, Ten Downing Street. Copies are to Lord Edward Stanley, Secretary of State for War, and Marques George Curzon, Foreign Secretary. In its essence, the Prime Minister charges Lieutenant General Percival-Trengove with three commands:

```
NO MATTER THE CIRCUMSTANCES DO NOT PAY
RANSOM STOP RESCUE THE HOSTAGES STOP DO
WHATEVER IT TAKES TO DESTROY THIS NOTO-
RIOUS BANDIT SUN MEI-YAO STOP NO QUES-
TIONS ASKED STOP I EXPECT EVERY MAN TO
DO HIS DUTY FOR KING AND COUNTRY STOP
GODSPEEED STOP PRIME MINISTER BALDWIN
```

池阝弓

Operations Room, British Legation, Shanghai International Settlement.
1600 hours, 23 May 1923

Lieutenant Colonel Roland Treadway, the Logistics Officer, says, "That's the entire troop movement plan. Any questions?" He looks about the room. "None? Best of luck, then."

Meanwhile, the Gurkhas board the cruiser, *HMS Suffolk,* at the Portland Dock. A corporal hauls their last machine gun on board. The sun dips below the horizon and the Officer of the Deck calls the bridge. "All aboard."

The navigator shouts to the longshoremen, "Cast off the fore line!" It splashes into the water and boatswain mates haul it on board.

"Cast off the aft lines."

The ship's twin screws turn slowly, and the cruiser eases into the Yangtze River, headed downstream. Within minutes, the cruiser is en route on its high-speed run to the Japanese Naval Base at Tsingtao, Shantung Province. Captain Ishihara Kanji has approved the *Suffolk's* port call.

Early the next morning, three Japanese trucks with their contingent of Gurkhas bounce along the road on the north side of the Patu-ku Mountains. A fourth truck follows, carrying Japanese marines and an intelligence officer.

他處.

Shanghai Railroad Station.
1800 hours, 23 May 1923

At sundown, the men of the Occidental brigade board two passenger-car trains. The trucks and other heavy equipment are on a freight train that follows. Sergeant Major McKenna checks each car, and confirms with the senior man on board that all is well. He gets confirmation from the conductor of the freight train that it is ready—all equipment is on board and secured.

McKenna shouts to the conductor, "Shove off."

The conductor waves his red flag overhead and blows a series of sharp blasts on his whistle. The engine's wheels scratch to gain traction. In a second or two, they gain purchase and the trains slowly begin their high-speed run to Lincheng. McKenna swings aboard the last car. He reflects, *Commander Stanhope-Owston is an excellent officer. He had requisitioned these trains by writ and now they are fully loaded and headed for battle.*

He recalls the commander's singular initiative in devising that aerial reconnaissance mission. *"Ding Hao,* Commander."

他處.

Bandit Sun's Hideaway, Shantung Province.
1800 hours, 23 May 1923

Sergeant Tang Tse-che reports to Captain Chao. "Sir, with your permission, I will go with the relief guards to our back entrance. The Datsun is serviced."

Engrossed with other concerns, Chao snaps, "Very well."

Chao returns to the radio room and finds Ch'uan Feng working assiduously to find a way around the jamming. "Success?"

"No, sir. That British jammer truly is the devil."

他遠.

Radio Room, British Legation, Shanghai International Settlement.
1830 hours, 23 May 1923

Chief Petty Officer James Cotterile opens the envelope marked SECRET that the general handed him two hours ago. With deliberate care, he encodes the words and taps the telegraphic key in his unique rhythmic style:

```
TO   PRIME   MINISTER   STANLEY   BALDWIN:
MY TROOPS AND I ARE EN ROUTE TO LINCHENG
BY TRAIN STOP TOMORROW WE MAKE CAMP AND
PREPARE STOP ON THE TWENTY-FIFTH WE WILL
LAUNCH OUR ASSAULT ON THE BANDIT SUN'S
HIDEOUT STOP PROGRESS REPORTS TO FOLLOW
```

他遠.

Gurkhas' Position in the Plain, Patu-ku Mountains.
1930 hours, 23 May 1923

By early evening, the Gurkhas have established their emplacement on the plain, facing the mountains and Sun's formidable defenses. In the moonless night, their patrol scouts the area and moves, deathly silent, behind the closest bandit machine-gun redoubt. The only sound heard is the swishing of their kukri knives. The Gurkhas strip the headless four-man crew of their weapons and steal the machine gun and its four ammunition boxes. The Senior Corporal whispers, "Tomorrow morning, Sun and his bandits will see our calling card and know that the Gurkhas will extract a terrible revenge for the massacre of our brothers-in-arms on the Shanghai Express."

他處.

Bandit Sun's Hideaway, Shantung Province.
2000 hours, 23 May 1923

Sergeant Tang Tse-che stumbles into the Operations Room. His right arm hangs limp. He grabs a chair and falls into it. Blood covers most of his clothing, which is tattered and smells of burnt cotton. He murmurs, "Mines. Lots of mines." His head falls to his chest. "I am cold. Very cold."

Captain Chao shouts for a corpsman. "Sergeant Tang, medical help is coming." He offers a glass of water. "Can you drink this water?"

"Perhaps." Tang grasps the glass with his bloodied left hand. It slips to the floor.

Corpsman Li Yuan-hung says, "Captain Chao, to one side, please, sir."

"Of course."

Li and others move Sergeant Tang to a table. He makes an assessment of his patient and covers him with a light blanket. "Captain Chao, the sergeant needs a blood transfusion immediately. His right arm has a compound fracture, he has several serious wounds about his body, and parts of his back and legs are badly burned. We must get him to the dispensary, now." He dabs some ointment on one of the leg burns. "That deep gash in his right leg requires a surgeon's hand. Send a horseman to Chefoo to fetch a doctor if you care for this man's life."

Li prepares a morphine syringe and is poised to make the injection.

"Wait!" shouts Chao. "I must have Tang's report." He leans close to the sergeant's face. "Tang, tell me your story—as simply as you can."

"I shall give him half of the narcotic," responds the corpsman in a defiant tone.

In weak and staggering whispers, Sergeant Tang stumbles through his travails. "Our truck hit a mine in the back road. The explosion blew our truck into pieces. I was thrown clear. The driver and his guard were killed instantly. The other fellow, not seriously wounded, went into the birch trees to find a way around the trap. He tripped a booby trap. The blinding flash, deafening blast, and the ping of shrapnel hitting the truck's remains told his end." He pauses a few seconds and breathes deeply. "I'm cold and in terrible pain." He again pauses. "I passed out after the booby trap explosion. Some of that shrapnel hit me, I believe."

Li injects the morphine into Tang's right arm. He and his assistant place Tang on a stretcher and carry him to the dispensary.

Captain Chao briefs Sun about Sergeant Tang's report. "He is a courageous soldier. One of our best. Only the gods know how he returned."

Sun, seriously concerned, shouts, "It's those Gurkhas! Those dammed British Gurkhas!" His eyes narrow and his mouth tightens. "MI6 has blocked our escape. We are trapped." He pours Scotch into two tumblers. "Drink up, Chao. One cannot anticipate the malevolent guile of that Secret Intelligence Service." He swigs heartily. "Tomorrow is the twenty-fourth. The next day my ultimatum expires. What portends, Captain Chao?"

Chao slumps in his chair. The import of the Gurkhas' capture of their secret back road imbues his soul. He takes the liquor, stares at the dark amber liquid, and sees phantoms taunting him. *Many curses on my ancestors for such devilment.* He drains the glass. Dolefully he responds, "We will hang." He buries his face in his hands and murmurs incoherently about aerial reconnaissance, the cursed Englanders, and the duplicitous Gurkhas.

Sun, with assurance, says, "Maybe not, Chao. Maybe we will not hang." He retreats to his desk and begins to write.

Almost as if on a theatrical cue, Lieutenant Yang Hasi-peng bursts into the room. In an excited voice he nearly shouts, "General Sun! General

Sun! Look!" He shoves the Gurkha Kashmir hat towards Sun. "We are doomed!" he cries.

""Shut up, idiot." Sun rises, grabs Yang by his shirt, and pulls him close. "Now, calmly tell me, where did you find this Gurkha hat?

"Yes, sir," Yang almost shouts. "It was in our first machine-gun redoubt." He gags and sits without permission, puts his head between his hands, and emits a low moan of fear.

With increasing disquiet, Sun tells Yang, "Be not afraid of hob-goblins." He forces a tumbler of Scotch to the fellow's hands. "Drink deeply."

With shaky hands, Yang manages to take a few sips. Soon, he says, "I am better, sir."

"Very well. The hat. Tell me about that hat."

"As the officer on duty, I checked our redoubts. I entered Station One at the foot of the mountain. The four-man crew is beheaded. Blood is everywhere." He gags, slumps in his chair, and swallows a deep drink of the Scotch. "Our machine gun is gone! And that Gurkha hat was in its place."

Sun goes to the window and stares at the darkness.

18

General T'ien Chong-yu's Headquarters, Chefoo, Shantung Province.
1500 hours, 24 May 1923

The concubine kneels close to Commander Stanhope-Owston and with delicate grace slowly pours the Malayan black tea into the Ming green cup before him. He tries to ignore the woman. But that skintight cheongsam and thigh-high split reveal her exquisitely sensuous body.

She notices, flashes her black eyes toward him, and smiles softly.

General T'ien Chong-yu, Governor and Commander of the Provincial Army of Shantung Province, also notices and grins widely. "Very nice, not so? My *Qizi* trained her to near perfection." He sips his tea. "After our meeting, I give her to you as a token of my good faith with the honorable British government."

Stanhope-Owston fumbles a bit at the inapt offer. "I am honored that you would sacrifice such a prize possession. I wonder if it would not be a too-large imposition for me to accept? I must ponder the ramifications."

"Ponder as you please, commander. You have piqued my interest with tales of warlords and bandits. Although, I must admit that I am at a loss, so far, as to the purpose of your unannounced visit to my humble house. You have a proposition for me?"

Stanhope-Owston sips the tea and steals a glance at the nearby concubine. With deliberate care, he places the cup on the saucer. He responds, "Your tea is excellent." After a short, awkward pause, he says in his most diplomatic voice, "We know that Marshal Chang Tso-lin of the

Fengtien Clique holds you to account for the Shanghai Express disaster and for raising the ire of the Occidentals." He raises the teacup, takes a small sip, and makes eye contact. "One of our agents overheard the marshal say, 'It was imprudent for Sun to tweak the lion's tail. General T'ien is derelict for letting this international tragedy happen, and for not retaliating against the bandit Sun and his gang. As Governor of Shantung Province and Commander of the Provincial Army, T'ien has the responsibility to ensure order in his province.' Peiping is most dissatisfied, General. Most dissatisfied." Keeping a straight face, he continues. "Is there a change on the winds from the north?"

T'ien is keenly embarrassed that an Occidental knows his well-kept secret. *It is none of the English's business.* Realizing that no viable option is open, he fusses with his own teacup and then speaks. "Unfortunately, you speak the truth, Commander. I am at a loss how to rectify the Fengtien's displeasure. I am helpless."

Stanhope-Owston sips tea, and recalls their latest intercepts from Peiping. He continues more forcefully, "To anyone with eyes, it is obvious that you have not contained that bandit Sun. In fact, it is rumored that Marshal Chang believes you are in cahoots with the bandit and split his spoils."

The general drops his teacup, rises, and in a loud voice says, "Our meeting is over. I keep the woman."

Commander Stanhope-Owston rises and says, "As you wish, General T'ien." He gathers his belongings and heads for the door.

"Perhaps I am too hasty," offers the general. "I beg you to finish your tea. A thousand apologies for my ill manners." He bows gracefully, extends a hand palm up, and says, "Please sit. I will have my woman serve more tea, if you please." As if on a second thought, and as a final act of contrition, he speaks softly. "After we conclude our business this afternoon, may I offer you the privacy of one of my bedrooms and the concubine? She is tantalizing, not so? You will find her amazingly resourceful."

Blushing at the enticing offer, Commander Stanhope-Owston nonetheless says, "Unfortunately, I must decline your gracious offer. Shortly, I will join the brigade for our upcoming battle with Sun." He pauses for a moment. "Perhaps I might offer a palpable solution to ease your awkward predicament."

The general leans forward. "I am eager to understand your proposal."

"May I have your word of honor that all I say will be held close to your heart?"

With increasing fervor, the general replies, "May my ancestors betray me if I reveal your confidential words."

"Very well. I am empowered by His Royal Britannic Majesty's Government to make a mutually beneficial agreement between us in the matter of the bandit Sun Mei-yao."

Excited that the British might, pull his chestnuts out of the fire, as it were, the general blurts, "Please continue. I am impatient."

"Sun has demanded an outrageous ransom for his hostages. Additionally, he requires immunity for his men and himself, and insists that his entire bandit gang be integrated into your provisional army."

The general cries, "Outrageous! That gang of rabble in my army? It is impossible." He fumes with faux concern. He knows well that Sun's bandit gang is better trained and equipped than his inept army, and that Sun already does his unpleasant tasks—for a small fee, of course.

"Perhaps not. Here is the secret concord we offer. To show our good intentions, my government has authorized me to pledge 50,000 British pounds sterling and sanctuary in Hong Kong with a new identity for you—after all of Sun's hostages are safely in our control."

Intrigued, General T'ien says, "There is more? With the British there always is more, not so?"

Ignoring the general's comment, Stanhope-Owston continues, "The British negotiators will agree to pay Sun's ransom demands and concur with his immunity requirement. In turn, you will sign a declaration accepting Sun and his bandits into your army."

The general is silent as he ponders Stanhope-Owston's comments. "Your proposal is unclear. Again, I am at a loss to understand. You offer me a large bribe and safe haven to accept Sun into my army against my wishes—a task you know I cannot do. The Fengtien Clique would look askance and the winds would become a cyclone. And why do I need safe haven for a task I cannot do? It is a conundrum."

General T'ien motions to the concubine to kneel beside him and massage his forehead—now covered in perspiration. He begins to relax. "You talk in riddles, Commander Stanhope-Owston of His Majesty's Royal Navy." There is a long silence as the woman continues her massage. "Please to give me the key to your charade. With you British, the key is usually the secret part of the deal. Not so?"

"General T'ien, your savvy is discerning. Please ask the woman to leave. The British key is for your ears only."

Several minutes later, Stanhope-Owston concludes, "We will have a transport aeroplane ready for you at the aerodrome at Chefoo and the payment will be in a valise under your seat."

General T'ien guffaws for several seconds. "Indeed, Commander Stanhope-Owston, you are devilishly clever. Agreed, Englishman, agreed." With humor in his voice, he says, "To seal this arrangement, and to show my good faith, I insist that you accept my hospitality for the evening. We will have a good time, yes?" He grabs Stanhope-Owston's hand and shakes it vigorously. "We will have a fine dinner and drink excellent champagne." He pauses and beckons his concubine to return. "And we have entertainment. All very excellent."

The unexpected invitation flummoxes Stanhope-Owston. Unsure how to respond diplomatically, he decides on the most direct approach. "General T'ien, your offer is most gracious. Unfortunately, I must return to my unit. Please understand."

With his eyes glaring, T'ien questions. "You decline my excellent offer to seal our arrangement? Yes? No deal. Leave!"

All the reasons he should leave flash through Stanhope-Owston's mind. The collapsed deal prevails. Deciding quickly, he says, "Excuse me, General. My mind was confused. I am pleased to accept your excellent offer."

Smiling ear to ear, the general pats Stanhope-Owston on the back generously. "We will have a fine time." He motions to the concubine. "Show our guest to your rooms."

19

*The Plain, Base of the Patu-ku Mountains, Shantung Province.
Noon, 25 May 1923*

The tires spin in the soft meadow and emit a telling sound. Sergeant Major McKenna dashes to the bogged-down truck and orders nearby men to follow. On the sergeant's command, the driver revs the engine, and the men, working in unison, force the truck to leap free. The cacophony of the brigade moving into position extends throughout the plain: trucks rumbling; noncommissioned officers shouting commands; men digging trenches; soldiers charging their weapons and talking loudly to ease their apprehension.

Meanwhile, Sun and Chao inspect their defensive positions: trained bandits manning the machine-gun redoubts; snipers hidden in rocky crevasses; and two crack infantry companies guarding the rocky pass. Two platoons of infantry and a machine-gun squad guard the road to the rear entrance. The remainder of Sun's troops is in reserve. From his command post in a large furrow in the mountain, Sun watches the brigade's activities through high-powered binoculars. He issues an order through his battery-powered telephone and four of his snipers change position.

The chess pieces are set. The brigade has the first move.

他處.

Lieutenant General Heathcliff Percival-Trengove checks with his intelligence officer, Lieutenant Colonel Matthew Nash. "What do you make of it?"

Nash, a tall and brash fellow from the Bailiwick of Guernsey, shakes his head. "General, this is not going to be easy. The best I can determine is that Sun's men and his machine guns are in the positions the photographs showed. They contrived a highly effective killing field in this plain. Of course, from this distance, we cannot confirm with certainty."

"Very well. Keep me informed."

Percival-Trengove ignores the staff officer standing at his post. "What say you, Sergeant Major?"

McKenna drops the binoculars, studies the situation, and responds, "It's a tough call, General. Sun's men have the high ground and they are hidden in those rocks. Let's send patrols to both flanks of that mountain. We need current intelligence."

"Do it."

McKenna orders the Gurkhas and the British marines to form six-man patrols to scout their assigned areas—marines to the right, Gurkhas to the left. Almost immediately, Sun's snipers ping at the patrols. Fortunately, their fire is ineffective because the patrols are outside the limits of the rifles' range. McKenna, through his high-powered binoculars, watches the patrols scamper over the open plain.

Fire from a camouflaged machine gun rakes the marines in their diamond formation. Three fall immediately, and the remaining three go to ground and try to dig in. Another marine drops.

"Damn!" McKenna shouts, "Those bandits bushwhacked the marines." He grabs his Thompson submachine gun, and commandeers a passing Italian truck. "That way!" He points to the marines. "Floorboard this claptrap." He charges his Tommy gun. The resounding snap fills the cab. Within seconds, the bullets snap around the truck. One crashes through the windshield and hits the driver in the head. He falls away dead and the out-of-control truck tumbles over.

McKenna, shaken and bruised, climbs out. He starts to run to the marines' position. A bullet crashes into the calf of his left leg. He tumbles to the ground. He lies still for a moment. He pulls his knife out of its holster, cuts away his pants leg, and wraps it around the wound to arrest the bleeding. He checks the drum magazine on his Tommy gun and fires a short burst.

With adrenaline pumping fast, he begins running zigzag. Machine-gun bullets whiz by, others smash into the ground near his feet. Another bullet grazes his scalp and the wound gushes blood, which nearly blinds his left eye. He stumbles, regains footing, and charges again. "Damn it. I'll kill those sons-of-bitches," he yells. With all the resolve and energy he has left, he continues toward the bandit's position. When he's only fifty yards away, a bullet strikes his left shoulder, ripping bone. He collapses. With the last of his fortitude, he crawls forward and fires his Thompson. Within seconds, the bandit machine gunners are dead and McKenna faints over his weapon. The remaining two marines rush toward him.

The general has observed this heroic scene. He shouts orders to the mortar squad. "Aim left. Commence! Commence!" Within three rounds, they find the range. Thundering explosions and blinding flashes of hot metal sear the mountainside. The machine guns are quiet. "Cease fire." In a stronger voice, "Cease fire!"

An ominous quiet suffuses the plain.

Sun shouts over his field telephone, "Redoubts, report." Within a few seconds, all have reported a few men slightly wounded and no damage to our machine guns.

"Very well. Stay alert. The Brits are noted for chicanery."

An ambulance and a truckload of French naval infantry rush to the fallen marines and McKenna. Sporadic sniping begins. Fortunately, it's in-effective. The medics load McKenna and the wounded and dead British marines into the ambulance. Sniper fire increases and some of the bullets hit the vehicle; one hits the glass windshield and it explodes in a shower of glass shards. The driver's face and body are covered in blood, seeping from dozens of puncture wounds. He clears his eyes of the blood and shouts, "*Je vais bien*! Let's get the hell out of here."

"Ready!" shouts the senior medic. A few minutes later, the ambulance is behind brigade lines.

Lieutenant General Percival-Trengove enters the ambulance, and sees a medic treating one of his marines. The fellow, in obvious pain, gives the general a thumbs up. Percival-Trengove smiles. "Stout fellow." He lifts the blood-stained sheet from the unconscious McKenna. "My God, man!" He covers McKenna, and growls at the medical crew, "You get *my* Sergeant Major to our medical people in the hospital in Lincheng, *très vite*. If he dies, I will court-martial every damn one of you. Understand? I personally will form the hollow square and strip you of all military insignias." He slaps the back of the ambulance as it rushes away. "Godspeed, Prometheus."

The Gurkha first-sergeant approaches the general. "Permission to eliminate those machine guns, sir."

Pleased at the Gurkha's *élan*, he knows their motive is revenge and not patriotic volunteerism. "No, Sergeant. Not now. Later, when the entire brigade moves forward. I'm counting on the Gurkhas to wipe out the bandit's lead positions." He overlooks the assembly of his troops and orders his officers, "Prepare to advance."

The orders ring through the brigade down to the privates. There is thunderous movement as the men make ready. One of the British marines comments to his pal, "Well, this is it, ol' chum. I survived the battle of the Somme—just barely." Instinctively he rubs his left shoulder. He fixes the bayonet on his rifle. "Reckon I won't this time."

Lieutenant Colonel Matthew Nash is shocked that the general's staff officers have not objected to the folly of a frontal charge into a clear field of fire. He is appalled at the inanity of this general's order. "By your leave, General," he says forcefully, "do not order a charge over this open ground. The enfilade from the bandit's well-fortified positions will cut our troops to ribbons." Amazed that he had the audacity to question the general's orders, Nash continues in a compassionate voice, "Assuming that some of our men survive to Sun's pass, they could not advance into that narrow opening and would be wiped out."

"Colonel Nash, you are insubordinate," snaps the general. "Tend to your intelligence affairs."

Unrestrained by his superior officer's command, Nash blurts, "General, your charge would be Passchendaele all over again. How many men do we sacrifice for seven hostages?"

Lieutenant General Percival-Trengove looks at Lieutenant Colonel Matthew Nash with questioning eyes. He grabs the back of his neck and rubs intently. He studies the maps. "It's not so much saving the hostages as it is eliminating this Sun bandit and his gang, and sending a message to the other gangs that their time is over."

Nash pauses to reinvigorate his courage. "Consider the political ramifications of having a large casualty list at home and in foreign capitals, and the hostages murdered—as Sun has promised."

The general rubs the back of his neck again, and then responds, "Nash, thanks. The serious wounding of Sergeant-Major McKenna, the killing of three of my marines and that Italian driver have clouded my mind." He looks at his maps and taps his pencil on the table. "This is the twenty-fifth—Sun's deadline. Will he murder his hostages if we don't accede to his ransom demands? I think not. He wants our money."

Nash offers, "It's a medieval siege. We can't advance and Sun cannot escape. We could wait it out until the bandit's food and water expire. But that's not tenable because we don't know the content of his larder, and the politicians would not allow this stalemate to continue indefinitely."

"If I had heavy artillery and air support—no matter, we don't have them and we're not going to get them any time soon."

At that moment, a forward observer vigorously cranks his mobile telephone box and reports.

"Go ahead," responds an anonymous voice.

"There are three soldiers coming out of the pass carrying a large white flag."

"Who are they?"

"No clue. All I see through my binoculars are these three guys."

"Keep me informed."

Moments later, seven of the forward observers send identical reports.

"General, three men with a white flag are approaching our lines."

"Order a cease fire immediately."

The order passes quickly through the brigade. Men speculate on what those fellows have to say.

One French sergeant says to his squad, "Is it a perfidious gambit? The Huns were noted for this ploy in the Great War. I was at Verdun and saw it happen several times. *Merde!*"

The bandits halt about halfway between the mountains and the brigade lines.

General Percival-Trengove tells Lieutenant Colonel Nash, "Since you speak Mandarin, see what the blackguards want."

Nash places his Webley revolver on the command table, and says, "I'll see."

He walks at a deliberate pace and stops a few feet in front of Sun's men.

Chao, in his dress uniform, salutes Nash. "Welcome to the plains of the Patu-ku Mountains. Permit me to introduce myself, Captain Chao Tan-keng at your service. I hope that your journey from Shanghai was not too troublesome."

Nash does not salute bandits. "Cut the chatter. What do you want, bandit?"

"Please, Lieutenant Colonel Matthew Nash, intelligence officer, let us have a civil and mutually convivial meeting."

Nash is nonplussed that the bandit knows his name, rank, and that he is Lieutenant General Percival-Trengove's staff intelligence officer. Nash says, cavalierly, "Lunch is being served at the Officer's Mess. I must return quickly. What do you want?"

"Very well then. It's simple. A permanent cease fire. Agreement to our ransom demands. I shall review them for you to ensure precise communications. For Major John Starly, one million British pounds sterling. For the Americans, Van Halsted and his wife, 200,000 United States dollars in gold certificates. And for each of the four American college girls, it is 50,000 United States dollars in gold certificates. Immunity for all the bandits. And incorporation into General T'ien Chong-yu's Provincial Army of Shantung. Lastly, depart from our backyard."

"Nonsense!" snaps Nash. "Here's what we want: the seven hostages in excellent condition and the bandit Sun."

"Impossible."

"Those are our unswerving demands. We want the hostages, now."

Captain Chao responds angrily, "If you want the hostages, come and get them." He and his men start to walk back to the pass. He turns and shouts, "Should your soldiers attack again, we'll hang the three adult hostages and toss the American girls to our men for their pleasure. Then we'll hang them."

Nash does not reply. He returns to the command bunker and relays the bandits' demands to Lieutenant General Percival-Trengove. "Damn those slimy bastards," utters the general. "They have the ace of spades as their hole card. But we've got them cornered like the vermin they are." He reviews the map again and asks of no one in particular, "Have we got Sun's back door sufficiently blocked?"

Lieutenant Colonel Nash responds, "Yes, sir. There is a platoon of British naval infantry and a squad of the White Russian Volunteers reinforcing the Gurkhas."

"That'll keep the bastards contained."

Stanhope-Owston enters the command bunker and hears the general's rant. "General, I have information."

"Commander James Stanhope-Owston! Where the hell have you been? It's mid-afternoon. That damn bandit has us check-mated. What's going on?"

"May we speak in private? I have important intelligence. It's for your ears only."

The general's demeanor changes immediately at the prospect of a solution. "Follow me."

Huddled far from the command post, Stanhope-Owston says, "I have made a deal with General T'ien Chong-yu, Governor and Commandant of the Provincial Army of Shantung Province."

"Why? Who authorized you to negotiate with that rogue? Ever hear of the chain of command?"

"No one tasked me with making this deal. I did it on my own initiative."

"You are indeed a cheeky fellow. Ought to court-martial you." The general harrumphs several times. "Well, get on with it. I've a stalemate to break."

Stanhope-Owston says in a straightforward voice, "Here's the deal I made with General T'ien Chong-yu."

Several minutes later, a large smile grabs the general's face. "Damn! I'm glad you fellows are on our side. Well done, Commander. Well done, indeed."

20

Battleground, Plain of the Patu-ku Mountains, Shangtung Province. 0300 hours, 26 May 1923

Lieutenant General Percival-Trengove stares into the blackness of no-man's land. Plaguing his mind are the horrors he experienced at the Somme and Passchendaele. *Dear God, there has to be a rational solution to this stalemate.* Back to reality, he orders, "Deploy four snipers."

"*Si, Generale,*" snaps Silvestre Fiscella, the Italian first sergeant.

"If there's any monkey business, shoot to kill those bandits."

"*Il mio grande piacere, Generale.*"

The General cracks a small smile at the verve of the Italian soldiers.

他處.

Later that morning, Lieutenant Colonel Nash asks, "Any last instructions, General?"

"I abhor having to negotiate with scum like that bandit Sun. You have our final terms. Convince him to accept."

"Yes, sir."

At 0900 hours, Lieutenant Colonel Nash and two of his men begin walking to the midway point in the plain. Their white flag catches the morning breeze and unfurls.

All hands watch Nash moving closer to the center on the plain. *Will Sun's men honor Nash's white flag?* Lieutenant General Percival-Trengove observes apprehensively as his negotiating team moves deeper into no-man's land. *If those bastards open fire, I'll mortar them to Hades.*

At mid-field, Nash waits silently for the bandits to respond. Today, hidden in his boot is a small Beretta 9mm. *If I go, that wanker goes with me.*

Within a few minutes, Nash spots Captain Chao and his men exiting the pass and hoisting their white flag.

"Captain Chao, General Percival-Trengove has commissioned me to represent him in these negotiations, and he demands that I deal directly with Sun Mei-yao to ensure that communications are crystal clear—no misunderstandings."

Chao squints his eyes as if great thoughts engulf his mind. "I shall tell Sun."

"We will wait."

Thirty minutes later, Sun arrives. He wears his former army dress uniform, including a sword, with several medals pinned on his blouse. "Good morning, Lieutenant Colonel Nash. You know who I am, so no need for pleasantries." He places his arms akimbo. "You asked for this meeting. You have news for me?"

Nash does not comment on Sun wearing an army uniform that he does not deserve. He responds, "Perhaps we could reach a compromise that would satisfy both of our commands."

"Excellent! You Occidentals have agreed to meet my demands. What are the arrangements for payment of the ransom?"

"Not so. Your demands are far beyond reason. However, we recognize that some amount of payment is appropriate. We would offer four million Chinese dollars for the return of the hostages in good condition."

Sun's mouth drops agape. He blinks his eyes several times in disbelief. *The British are making a joke.* "I like you, Lieutenant Colonel Nash—a man with humor in his soul." He guffaws loudly. "I like your witticism—sets a productive ambiance for our talk."

"Bandit Sun, I offer no joke. Our offer is genuine."

Shocked at the outrageousness of the Occidental's offer, Sun narrows his eyes and his lips tighten. With anger, he spits, "You insult me. You know as well as I that the Chinese dollar is nearly worthless. Four million would purchase a bowl of rice, maybe. Get serious or this session is over."

"Very well, let's…"

他走.

Over the next hours, Nash and Sun dicker intensely. They are overheard by the attendants:

"You British are so loggerheaded."

"Let us stop this bloodshed—it bodes ill for both of us."

The bargaining continues, sometimes with odium and at other times with conviviality—each side moving nearer to closure.

Mentally exhausted, and knowing that in the long-term he will lose all, Sun says in a doleful voice, "Very well, Occidental. I accept."

"Excellent." Nash reviews the terms. "Sun, you agree that in exchange for one hundred thousand Mexican silver pesos, you will return all your hostages safely. Additionally, the Occidentals grant unlimited immunity to your men and you, and General T'ien Chong-yu will integrate your entire band into his Provisional Army."

"Yes, that is correct," Sun affirms in a dejected voice. *A pittance. At least I have avoided the hangman's knot.*

On a signal from Nash, four teams of two soldiers each carry heavy metal boxes which jingle loudly. The men place the boxes behind Nash. Without comment, they return to the Occidental lines.

Nash says, "These silver pesos are payable on delivery of the seven hostages and the Chinese Christian Sue Chen in excellent condition to the Occidental forces on this plain."

Surprised by this arbitrary demand for the Chen woman, Sun replies, "No! Sue Chen is not part of our bargain. She is my interpreter and I will take her for my number three wife. Absolutely not." A few seconds later he demands, "Englander, how do you know of my Sue Chen?"

Nash smiles faintly and responds, "Intelligence, bandit Sun. British Intelligence."

"You Occidentals are sons of Satan!" he spouts, and jabs his right index finger at Nash's chest. "No! I keep her. Understand?"

"Understand clearly, Sun, without Mistress Chen there is no deal."

"We did not discuss Chen in our bargaining." He jabs his finger at Nash. "You British are devils on this earth."

"If you do not agree, we'll take these silver pesos back to our lines and we'll continue our siege."

Sun snaps, "The hostages will be dead."

"Within two days, we will have heavy artillery and air power. And, your men, as they lie wounded and dying, will wonder why you did not complete our bargain, and you will meet your ancestors in the hangman's noose."

The defeated Sun drops his head, and mumbles, "Once again, you deceitful Occidentals foist another unequal treaty on the Chinese by the power of the gun."

Nash orders, "Bring the hostages and Mistress Chen here to conclude this deal in peace."

Almost on cue, General T'ien Chong-yu and his heavy-weapons battalion—his elite troops—arrive on the field and without fanfare deploy in parade formation. He sends a runner to Sun with welcoming greetings.

Single file, the hostages and Sue Chen emerge from the pass. Six of Sun's men escort them onto the field. Viewing the scene, they sense that deliverance is near, and they begin chatting happily. Sun commands that his prisoners form a straight line and face the Occidentals. He draws his Mauser pistol and points it at the prisoners. He shouts, "I know how devious you British are. Should you betray me, I will murder my hostages," he says with cool precision. His men draw their weapons and aim at the hostages.

Nash says, "No deception, Sun. Just the deal we agreed to." Nash, with unabashed bravado, goes to the hostages and says forcefully, "Follow me. Say nothing. Do not look back."

With smiles all around, and a few tears, the hostages begin walking at Nash's deliberate pace toward the Occidental lines. A runner from the

Occidentals' line hands a leather purse to Sue Chen. She distributes letters from home. Medical personnel greet the captives and hustle them to the medical tents.

Sun beckons the men from the nearest machine-gun emplacement to retrieve the metal boxes and return them to his headquarters. Climbing the rock stairs with the heavy boxes is a challenge. One soldier slips and the box tumbles down the steps toward the plain. The latch snaps open and the rocks inside spill helter skelter.

General T'ien Chong-yu beckons Sun forward. Sun is elated that he has fulfilled his scheme to full measure. A surge of brash haughtiness envelops his being. Soon he will be a commissioned officer in a regular army, the ransom is ample, and his neck will not be fit to a hangman's noose. He marches in quick time to greet General T'ien.

Sun greets General T'ien with a snappy hand salute and says, "I am pleased to join your splendid army."

"Welcome, Colonel Sun—your rank in my army." He hands Sun two shoulder boards; on each, three gold oak leaves are arrayed symmetrically on an emerald-green background. "You are pleased?" Without waiting for an answer, he hands Sun a brand-new American rifle. "I have these American Springfield model M1903, caliber 30-06 rifles for your men and each has a bayonet and scabbard. For your officers and non-commissioned officers, I have Thompson submachine guns and Colt 45 pistols. All are surplus from the Great War, but not used." He motions to his staff and two men bring the additional weapons to Sun. T'ien cracks a huge smile. "These new weapons are for your excellent recruits into my Provisional Army."

Sun inspects the weapons and salutes General T'ien Chong-yu. With glee in his voice he responds, "Yes, General T'ien, these are very fine weapons. We are pleased to join your army." He is enthralled by his good fortune. *Now, it is I who will hunt and kill Mandarin Fu and seize his black empire.*

"Order your men to throw away their antiquated weapons and enjoy new American arms."

Sun sends a runner to Captain Chao with the order.

Moments later, a stream of his men file onto the plain and stack their rifles. Soon, all of the bandits are on the plain. To show General T'ien and the British how well trained his gang is, Sun orders them to fall into formations in front of the mountains. Four companies of troops form in near-perfect military order. Chao stands proudly in front of Sun's bandit army. "Forward march!" he shouts.

The bandits march in synchronization toward General T'ien's army.

About fifty yards in front of them, Chao calls, "Halt."

All stand stiffly at attention. Sun faces General T'ien and gives a snappy salute. "We are ready to join General T'ien Chong-yu's Provisional Army."

General T'ien returns the salute. He draws his Mauser pistol. A single bullet hits Sun in the forehead and he drops to the ground without life. A Nepalese sniper fires and Captain Chao falls with a bullet in his heart. General T'ien's men fix bayonets and aim at Sun's men. Bewildered by their leaders' murders, Sun's soldiers scatter in disarray.

A Russian sniper, hidden in a low crevice in the mountain, observes the unfolding scene through his binoculars. He raises his rifle, looks through the telescopic finder, and makes a fine adjustment. He focuses on his target, takes a deep breath, and squeezes the trigger. The rifle kicks. General T'ien looks bewildered as blood gushes from the hole in his chest. He kneels, falls forward, and greets his ancestors.

Commander James Stanhope-Owston surveys the brutal scene through his binoculars and waxes plaintively, "That ought to assuage the Fengtien Clique and convince them to leave the British lion alone." He walks away. *I wonder who will care for General T'ien's concubine?*

EPILOGUE

Throne Room, Buckingham Palace, London.
1000 hours, 16 October 1924

The band plays "God Save the King." Stanley Wilkerson, father of Karina Ashley-Cooper, stands on the honors' carpet. He is in full mourning dress: black morning coat, grey waistcoat, grey cashmere striped trousers, and winged-collar white shirt.

The Earl of Ancaster, Gilbert Heathcote-Drummond-Willoughby, The Lord Great Chamberlain, taps his great white stick three times. The sounds in the Throne Room fade to quiet. He announces, "His Royal Britannic Majesty, King George the Fifth. God save the King."

The King enters the room, looks about, and sees that all is ready. He speaks in a thunderous voice, "Good morning. Today we honor those who, with exceptional bravery and courage, have fought for King and Country." The King opens the small brown jewelry case in his hand and says, "To Karina Ashley-Cooper, née Wilkerson, posthumously, I invest the George Cross for exceptional valor and self-sacrifice in the presence of the enemy in defense of the Empire. Mister Wilkerson, accept this investiture for your courageous daughter."

Wilkerson steps forward and, with tears in his eyes, accepts the box containing the medal and ribbon. He mumbles, "Thank you, Your Majesty." He bows his head slightly. A few minutes later, King George says, "To Major Quentin Ashley-Cooper, Royal Marines, posthumously, I invest the Victoria Cross for conspicuous gallantry and self-sacrifice in face of the enemy in defense of the Empire."

Wilkerson also accepts the investiture for his son-in-law because Quentin had no close, living relatives.

The Lord Great Chamberlain, with an almost-invisible signal, urges Master Sergeant Shaun McKenna to come forward. With his shoulders erect and head high, he walks forward with a just-perceptible limp. The left sleeve of his uniform hangs empty. The array of medals on his dress-blue uniform clicks in a harmonious tone. He stands stiffly at attention in front of the King. His Majesty smiles faintly and says, "Master Sergeant Shaun McKenna, Marine of the United States of America, I invest the Victoria Cross for exemplary valor, and conspicuous gallantry. With total disregard for your own safety, and sustaining three life-threatening wounds, you rescued a squad of British marines pinned down by enemy machine gun fire."

The king says with a smile, "I see no room on that broad chest to pin this medal, Master Sergeant." He hands the opened brown case containing the award to McKenna. "It is my privilege to make this investiture to you, my American cousin."

McKenna takes the award in his right hand, and speaks in a soft voice, "Thank you, Your Majesty." If one were to look closely at the sergeant, one might see small tears on his cheeks.

The Commandant of the Marine Corps, Major General John S. Lejeune, watches intently. As McKenna returns to the gallery, General Lejeune renders a snappy salute.

"Master Sergeant McKenna, congratulations. You've done the Corps and our country proud. I am recommending you for the Navy Cross, your third award."

"Thank you, General."

Another signal from the Lord Chamberlain causes the mother and father of Miles Prichard to advance toward the king. He speaks in a low, personal voice, "My deepest sympathies for the loss of your son." Then, in his normal voice, he announces, "For exceptional valor in service of the Empire in face of hostile fire, I award Colour-Sergeant Photographer, Reserve, Miles Prichard, posthumously, the Order of the British Empire." He hands the medal and ribbon to Mister Prichard. Missus Prichard holds back her sobs, a true Briton.

Margaret Jasperson stands on the knight's carpet. She is dressed in a pale blue, light wool dress trimmed in white, and wears a matching, wide-brimmed cloche hat with a bow. King George says, "For exceptional service to the Empire, in manifestly hazardous circumstances, I dub you Margaret Jasperson, Dame of the Empire, Order of the Garter."

他處.

With her cover exposed, MI6 executives now assign Margaret Jasperson to Headquarters in Broadway House, London. There, she quickly rises to ever-increasing responsibilities. In 1937, the Secretary of State for Foreign Affairs, Anthony Eden, appoints her Chief of the Secret Intelligence Service (MI6). On 8 November 1939, while walking out of a cinema screening a rerun of the 1932 film *Shanghai Express,* she is pricked by the umbrella tip of an Oriental man with a French accent. She dies shortly thereafter of curare poisoning.

他處.

Commander James Stanhope-Owston, Royal Navy, is given a number of increasingly responsible assignments, including Captain of the battleship *HMS Warspite.* The Admiralty commissions him Rear Admiral in 1940. During World War II, because of his extensive service in China, the Admiralty assigns him to General Chang Kai-shek's command as the British liaison officer in Chunking. During an intense Japanese air raid on 23 August 1943, Rear Admiral Stanhope-Owston is killed when a bomb makes a direct hit on his bunker.

他處.

Cholmondeley Alastair resigns from the Secret Intelligence Service shortly after the Shanghai Express episode is concluded. He remains in China as a freelance intelligence agent working for any government, warlord, or emblematic group that meets his pay demands.

Shortly before World War II starts in September 1939, Major General Sir Stewart Graham Menzies, head of the Secret Intelligence Service, recalls SIS agent Cholmondeley Alastair to London and assigns him to the Special Operations Executive, a super-secret organization with unscrupulous credentials. Alastair successfully executes a number of operations against the Empire of Japan and other unnamed entities.

On his retirement in 1946, Alastair moves to a quiet village in East Anglia where he later dies peacefully of old age. In 2001, MI6 finally releases his biography, *Double Agent in China*. It becomes a runaway bestseller—much to the embarrassment of several governments, friendly and not so.

他處.

Army Headquarters names Lieutenant General Heathcliff Percival-Trengove Governor of the Punjab on the Indian Frontier. In 1924, he leads the Second Punjab Regiment into the Northwest Frontier on a Dacoit-suppression mission. These thugs had raided numerous villages, killing and robbing the Indian occupants. A sniper's bullet hits him in the chest and he falls from his horse, dead.

他處.

Laura Todd does not remarry. She returns to China in 1925 and establishes the Wellspring Mission in Ye-an in Sanshi Province. It thrives under her sterling leadership. In October 1937, the Japanese Kwangtung Army ransacks her mission and kills her while she is defending the children in her care.

他處.

By October 1925 Ralph and Maureen Van Halsted had expired. To this day, we have no evidence that her jewels were recovered.

他處.

Neither Nani Atticus' valise nor Xenia De Luca's body are ever found. However, peasants find the bodies of Mahima Rahman, Mae Ling-weh, Monique Harmonie, and Bridget von Cairo. They strip the bodies of clothing, shoes, and whatever else they can scavenge. The wild dogs feast, and over time the bones are scattered.

他處.

The five collegiates collaborate on a book that recounts their adventures. Thea, by default, is the lead editor. Overnight, their book becomes a bestseller, as the public is eager for authentic details of their harrowing experience in remote China. United Artist Pictures purchases an option on the book and produces an epic film that is a smash hit. Thea plays herself, masterfully evoking intense sympathy in audiences. With her slightly crooked smile, Thea becomes one of Hollywood's most accomplished and popular actresses.

Bonny, Mindy, Bertie, and Melinda complete their degrees, marry into wealthy families, raise their children, and live to ripe old ages.

他處.

Rumors ran rampant regarding Prudence's disappearance. She is never found.

END

PHOTOGRAPHIC GALLERY

I have posted the following photographs according to when the subject was first mentioned.

Chapter One

Gurkha Soldiers

Shanghai Express

Chapter Two

Sikh Guard

Gurkha Kasmir Hat

Gurkha Kukri Knife

Mao Tse-Tung, Leader of
the Chinese Communist
Party

International Settlement,
Shanghai, 1920s

Chapter Three

Ted Weems,
Orchestra Leader

Victrola Gramaphone

Chapter Ten

President of the USA,
Warren G. Harding

British Prime Minister Sir
Stanley Baldwin, KC, PG

Chapter Eleven

Sun Yat-sen,
Generalissimo of the
Chinese Kuomintang
Party

Charles Evans Hughes,
Secretary of State of the
USA

Marques George Curzon,
KG, GCSI, British Foreign
Secretary

Dino Grandi, Italian
Minister of Foreign
Affairs

Raymond Poincaré,
French Minister for
Foreign Affairs

Captain Sir Mansfield
George Smith Cumming,
KCMB, CG

James Ramsay MacDonald,
Member of Parliament,
Labour Party

Chapter Twelve

Chapter Fifteen

Bristol F2b, Two-Seater Fighter

Carl Crow, Red Cross
Shanghai

Chapter Thirteen

Leica Model "O" 35mm Camera

Lord Edward George
Derby, British Secretary of
State for War

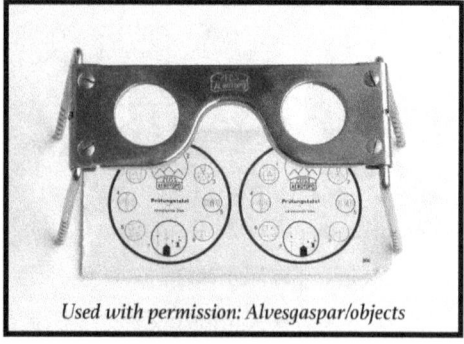

Stereoscopic Viewer

Chapter Sixteen

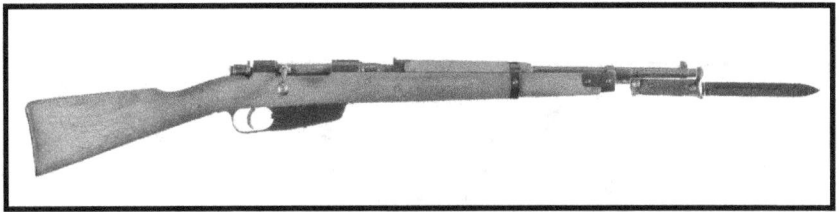

Italian Carcano Rifle with Bayonet

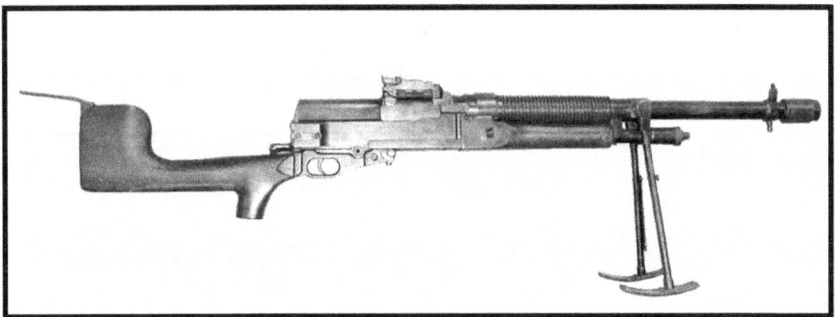

M 1922 Hotchkiss Machine Gun

Chapter Eighteen

General T'ien Chong-yu

Chapter Twenty

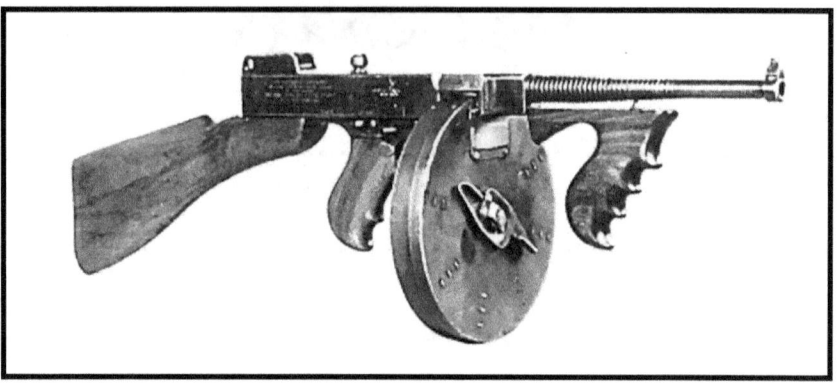

Thompson Submachine Gun

Mexican Silver Peso, Circa 1920s

ABOUT THE AUTHOR

Captain S. Martin Shelton retired from active and reserve naval service. He served in the Korean and Vietnamese Wars. He has an extensive background in Far Eastern studies.

Shelton earned his Master of Arts Degree (Cinema) from the University of Southern California. He spent thirty years producing a host of information and documentary motion-media shows, winning over forty awards in national and international film competitions and festivals. Shelton is a Fellow of the Society for Technical Communication and of the Information Film Producers of America.

Shelton has published extensively in trade magazines, peer-reviewed journals, and commercial publications. His professional book, *Communicating Ideas with Film, Video, and Multimedia,* garnered the Best of Show award in the Society for Technical Communication's Spotlight Publication Competition.

He published the action-adventure novel, *St. Catherine's Crown* in 2013. This narrative describes the harrowing adventures of the Grand Duchess

Anastasia and her cousin, Lieutenant Kirik Pirogoff, during the Russian Revolution and regicide of the royal family, and then post-Revolution as they travel along the Trans-Siberian Railroad to refuge in northwestern China.

Following, he published the anthology titled, *Aviators, Adventures, and Assassins.* Included are two novellas. *Amelia* is the investigative journal of a naval intelligence officer unraveling the skullduggery of Amelia Earhart's last leg of her around the world flight in July 1937. *Prester John* details a Christian knight's two-decade long search for a chimerical king. Also included are several dozen short stories.

His novella titled, *Khartoum* earned a Finalist award in the Writer's League of Texas Annual Publication Competition in 2013. Set during the Madhi's Muslim capture of the Anglo-Egyptian Sudan in 1898, the story describes the harrowing adventures of two German siblings trying to escape up the Blue Nile to Ethiopia.

His novel titled, *Abyssinia* earned a Finalist award in the Indie National Excellence Book Awards. The narrative is set during the Italian Fascist's occupation of Ethiopia in 1937. A female Italian archaeologist and an American intelligence agent find damming evidence that the Italians used poison gas in their conquest. Dogged by the Secret Police, they try to escape to a friendly country.

Shelton's web site address is www.sheltoncomm.com

www.ingramcontent.com/pod-product-compliance
Lightning Source LLC
Chambersburg PA
CBHW060110260626
47160CB00005B/1847